RESTLESS FROM THE START

By: Joei Carlton Hossack

Skeena Press
P. O. Box 19071
Sarasota, Florida 34276-2071

Restless From The Start

Library of Congress Catalog Card Number
97-091654

ISBN 0-9657509-0-6

Published by Skeena Press
P.O. Box 19071
Sarasota, Florida 34276-2071

Printed in the United States of America by
Independent Publishing Co.
P.O. Box 18566
Sarasota, Florida 34276

RESTLESS FROM THE START

TABLE OF CONTENTS

Restless From The Start

The Piece of Paper

"Where's Harry?" asked my mother, as she walked to the door, opened it and looked out onto the street, in both directions.

"I dunno," I answered, "I came here by myself."

"How did you get here?" my mother asked.

"I took two buses," I told her, puffing out my chest, rather proud of myself.

My mother ignored me and went back to work for a few minutes, before asking again. "Where's Harry?"

"I dunno, he didn't come home, so I asked Mrs. Greer how to get here on the bus," I said, handing my mother the piece of paper with the directions on it.

I was five years old. There wasn't a label for it, at the time; but, today, I would be called a "latch key" kid. My father worked at the fruit and vegetable terminal and auction, full time, in addition to owning his own grocery store for awhile. I cannot ever remember my mother not working. She either made and beaded hats in a factory, or worked in my father's store, or both. My oldest brother, Nathan, ignored me totally. My brother, Harry, was my favorite. He was my babysitter, my protector, my idol and the wildest fifteen year old on the street. Harry was the person I looked to for ideas. My sister, Mona, and I fought constantly.

Harry was supposed to be around, someplace close to the house, and he wasn't. I asked a neighbor, Mrs. Greer, where my parent's store was located. She knew the address and the telephone number of the store. Since Mrs. Greer often prepared lunch for me during school days, a necessity that my mother paid for, and occasionally, took care of me after school, when my parents were very late, this information was close at hand. On this particular day, I asked her for the directions.

I don't think Mrs. Greer, would, for one minute, assume that I would use those directions to go looking for the store. But I did. I followed them exactly. I walked to the corner, and waited for, and got on, the correct bus. Since the directions were written out, the bus driver told me where to change buses. After getting off the second bus, again thanks to the directions that were neatly written out, the driver pointed me in the right direction, to walk the half block to my parent's store. I walked into the store so proud of myself.

That piece of paper might have been the start of my mother's heart problems.

I know this was the beginning of my spirit of adventure. I have always been Restless From The Start.

A Time Remembered

How wonderful that a word, or a gesture, or even just a moment of quiet reflection, will conjure up a memory of so long ago.

My family was not religious. Dinner Friday nights, were the same as any other night, and although both my brothers had their Bar Mitzvah, they did not attend regular Friday night or Saturday services. Holidays, however, were another matter. They were a reason to get together with family--brothers, sisters, cousins, aunts and uncles.

Passover, 1950,
Montreal, Canada

I am the baby of the family, aged 6, Mona is 11, Harry, the devil, is 16 and Nathan is 18. I always sat next to my favorite brother, Harry. Harry, the brother who taught me to ride his bicycle. The same brother who taught me to sing like Johnny Rae, by going down on one knee, and who took me to baseball games. Harry, who worked on the train as a news agent and took me along with him, to Cornwall, Ontario, from time to time. The same brother, Harry, who was now whispering in my ear "I'll give you a dime for every glass of wine you drink." He poured, I drank. My parents never noticed. Just before my head went down on the table and passing out, I thought I heard my mother yelling something.....

Could that have been the time, we discovered that red wine produces the migraine headaches, that I have been plagued with for over forty-five years? I hope not; but, I still maintain Harry owes me 60 cents, PLUS interest. He doesn't remember.

Do We Ever Change?

When Abraham, was told by his God, to sacrifice his son Isaac, we know one thing for sure. Isaac was not a teenager at the time. Had he been, it would not have been called "sacrifice". It would have been called "justifiable homicide". I was that kind of teenager.

I won't describe the fist fights I got into, or the foul language I used in school, or the ditching of school in favor of an afternoon movie or the smoking or the always threatening to run away from home; however, only I could get away with such nonsense. A) being the baby of the family, helped; B) my parents spoiled me rotten and C) I could pull a migraine headache out of the air, so whatever I did, I was never reprimanded. "Don't yell - she'll get sick" was always on my mother's lips.

The incident I am about to relate, occurred when I was fifteen years old. I had an exceptionally smart mouth at the time, and at 5'9", I towered over my mother.

Much to the relief of my parents, I had spent six weeks, during that summer, visiting my sister in California. I experienced my first real taste of freedom. While Mona worked all day, I had the run of her apartment. When her future husband, Marv, needed a rest from law school, he picked me up and took me to the beach, otherwise, I had the days to myself. I had met everyone, in the two story apartment building, at the swimming pool - something only dreamed about in Montreal, Canada, and had experienced my first major crush, on a twenty-two year old blond, hunk, named Bruce.

My parents arrived in the last week of my vacation. We were all going to attended the wedding of my sister and her fiancé, and on the day after the wedding, my parents and I, would be going back to Canada. At that time Mona and Marv could embark on married life and leave on a short honeymoon.

That's when the problem started. My parents wanted to book our return flight to Canada and I calmly announced that I would sooner be caught dead, then fly home with them. "I'm taking a bus," I said coolly.

"You are flying with us," my mother insisted.

"I'm not going," I retorted.

To make a short story, even shorter, after the wedding and just before they flew home, my parents delivered me to the Greyhound Bus Terminal in downtown Los Angeles. Another "win" for the mouth, for what they would describe, to their friends back home as, a grueling three day and four night, trip through hell.

Personally, it was heaven. The changes in the scenery from big city, to country, to wide open spaces, were thrilling. The people, from all parts of America, were exciting. It was wonderful being on my own and on the following morning, after a very restless night sleep, I loved walking around the western town of Rock Springs, Wyoming.

My love affair ended abruptly. I returned to find that I had been walking too long and the bus had left without me. My luggage remained secure in the belly of the bus and some hand luggage, had been left in the overhead rack, above seat number twenty-eight.

Horrified, I sat down to have a cup of coffee and gather my thoughts. Even in those days, I was a coffee drinker. Wild thoughts went through my mind. " What would Harry do, in this situation?" I thought. By this time, you know that Harry is my (forever getting me into trouble, like I can't do it well enough, on my own) brother, ten years older than myself. It came to me in a flash. "Hitchhike, or course!"

With the help of a waitress in the restaurant, who called the Greyhound Head Office, I learned that the next stop was two hundred and sixty miles away in Cheyenne, Wyoming. I called the bus depot in Cheyenne and asked if they would take all my luggage, including what I had stowed over seat number twenty-eight, off the bus and I would be there as soon as I could. Even the Greyhound dispatcher, did not dare ask how I was going to get there "as soon as I could".

The year was 1959 and the highways and byways of middle America, were a little safer. Although I looked much older, women were considered less of a threat and since the car that stopped for me had a couple of youngsters in it, perhaps the couple recognized my long thin legs and lanky body as that of a teenager, despite my height. Their children were only a few years younger than myself.

The thrill of hitchhiking was over. The two hundred and sixty mile trip was totally uneventful. We played games in the back seat. Mr. and Mrs. Wilder treated me to a burger and fries lunch and when we approached Cheyenne, they asked if I would like to continue with them to Rome, New York. I thanked them and declined their kind offer. In Cheyenne, my luggage was waiting at the Greyhound Bus Depot. The station master rerouted my ticket. I got on another bus almost immediately.

No one would be wiser, unless I told the story.....and I told the story to everyone, including my horrified parents.

The rest of the "ordeal", as my parents liked to call it, was a breeze and memories of that trip, my first trip, remains one on the highlights of my early days. If my parents were alive today, they would be in a constant state of shock over my escapades.

I have remained the same. I still take long bus rides. I still miss flights, buses and trains. I still love talking to strangers. I am still intrigued by new places and, my friends tell me, that I still have the same "smart mouth".

In my mind, I am still that 15 year old girl.

The wonderful thing about a Date From Hell, is that it doesn't matter how many years go by, that Date remains fresh in your mind, like it happened yesterday. This story took me back to the 1960's.

Does This Product Have a "Best If Used Before" Date?

"No, I'm sorry, I don't understand." "Brian told you, I was a bitch and the worst date he's ever had, and you wanted to see for yourself?" "Are men really from this planet?" I thought.

When I would return to Montreal, Canada, from my newly adopted home in Los Angeles, California, there would be a flurry of activity from my friends and family. Who could introduce me to "that special someone" so I would change my plans and stay in Canada?

To that end, nobody even came close; however, I usually enjoyed the string of dates that were arranged for me. The guys were always eager to meet a "California girl" - even if she did work in an office and had no plans on going into show biz.

I had left my home in Montreal, Canada, at the age of eighteen and was now in my early twenties. I was tall, slender, dark haired, and had a natural streak of gray hair at the front. I had developed a quick wit and a very sharp tongue, so I could banter with the best of them.

"Hello Shirley, this is Marc, a friend of Rhonda's," a pleasant sounding voice said, through the telephone wires. "Oh, hi," I replied, "any friend of Rhonda's is a friend of mine." "Haven't seen her this week, what's she doing?" I asked.

"The usual," came the reply, "just rehearsing for a

play".

Rhonda should be in Hollywood, I thought, not me. She had the face of a porcelain doll and loved theatrics.

"Rhonda said that you'll be here just a few more days." "Want to grab a bite to eat and go to a show tonight?" he asked. "I'd love to, great, see you later." "At 6:00," Marc replied, getting the address and directions, before hanging up the phone.

I was pleasantly surprised when I opened the door. He was taller than me. That in itself would have made the date a success, since I was 5'9" and towered over most of my friends and their beaux. He was rather good looking, even though he was dark haired, while I preferred blonds. He seemed, also, to have an easygoing and pleasant manner, to add to his other qualities. Even before he opened the car door for me, we were in a conversation.

"Nice car," Shirley commented, "what year?"

"1963," Marc replied, "gets me where I want to go."

"And where do you want to go?" I asked.

"How about Schwartz's, for smoked meat, and then, Where The Boys Are?"

"Rhonda must have told you that the smoked meat in L.A. was awful." "Thanks, that sounds great," Shirley responded enthusiastically.

Dinner was delightful and we had no trouble making conversation at the table. The movie was mediocre and coffee, afterwards, was enjoyable.

"Now what the hell are you talking about? " I asked. "I don't understand how Brian got into our conversation." "Brian," I asked mystified, "the jerk I went out with last week?" "He's a friend of yours?" "The guy is a moron," I said, my voice becoming a little shrill and my sentences starting to run together.

"Brian told me, you were the worst bitch he had ever met." "I told him, I wanted to see for myself, how bad you were - but," said Marc, "I had a terrific time." "What happened with Brian?"

"He's got a new job," I replied, most annoyed at being reminded. "He's in sales now." "He spent the entire evening trying to sell me one of his products.....a cemetery plot." I told him, "since I had no intentions of living here....I sure as hell, wasn't going to die here." "Fortunately," I continued, "he had just pulled into my driveway, I said good night and slammed the door." "That was the last conversation I had with your friend, the hotshot salesman."

Marc put his arms around me and squeezed me, ever so slightly, as we both shook our heads in disbelief. "Oh, Christ," Marc said, suddenly trying to control his laughter, "it was fun. Thanks. Have a safe trip back to California."

The Wheel of Misfortune

I have had one ticket in my thirty-four years of driving. It was for speeding. I was driving 43 miles per hour in a 35 mile per hour zone and even that ticket might have stemmed from the fact that, upon being shown the radar equipment, I said "Oh, is that the little gizmo that clocked a tree doing 60 on last Saturday's news?" "No, Ma'am," said the officer, in a controlled and authoritative voice, as he wrote out the ticket. I have never felt the urge to speed since that time.

I also must confess to six or seven automobile accidents, but I have never been in the various cars, when they were hit. The cars have always been parked, and parked legally. So why, do I know so many people, whose driving scares the hell out of me?

My five foot tall, red headed, mother, did very little driving. She was only permitted, by my father, to drive on very straight roads, for extremely short periods of time and only when the weather was clear and pleasant. On one of these occasions, she was stopped by the Highway Patrol for driving about 10 miles per hour in a 50 mile per hour zone. The officer asked if she had gotten her license in a "Cracker Jack" box and asked to see it. That was when she learned that her sex was listed as "male" on her driver's license. She never drove again.

My father did almost all of the driving and being a passenger in his car, could be construed as torture. He was a terrible driver. The trip that stands out the clearest, in my mind, took place in 1974. That was the year I had a rather debilitating skiing accident. My knee had to be pinned and stapled back together, so I dared not risk the three hundred and fifty mile drive from Montreal, Quebec, Canada to Boston, Massachusetts, by myself.

My father, his wife Celia, and I, picked up a cousin and her husband and we were off, leaving home around 6:00 A.M.. Four hours later, and sixty miles away, just over the American border, we stopped for coffee. The next words out of my father's mouth drove me to the brink of insanity. "And in two hours," he said "we'll stop for lunch". "In two hours," I shrieked "we won't even be in Plattsburg and that thirty miles away". "How about taking a nap, Pa, I'll drive for a while" I said through teeth, clenched so tightly, my jaw ached. We traded places. He climbed into the back seat and I limped to the driver's side and parked myself behind the steering wheel. It didn't take ole Fred long to fall asleep.

He awoke agitated. "I can't sleep when you drive," he said. "Where are we?" "Just outside of Boston, Pa," I replied. Needless to say, I was recruited to drive the return trip as well.

My husband; however, was the worst. He was so sure of himself, that he loved to test his reflexes behind the wheel of his car. For every ten miles of speed, he felt an inch or two behind the car in front, was sufficient. His tailgating terrified me and more than once, we found ourselves on two wheels, pulling into another lane, so as not to smash ourselves into the car in front.

On a humorous note, and there were very few humorous notes, while we were commuting to and from work, we picked up my sister from the airport. We drove her to my brother's house. Paul pulled into his driveway. Since Nathan's car was already in the driveway, the back end of our car, was still on the side walk. "Pull up, Paul.....closer..... closer, pull up," said my sister. "Come on Paul," said Mona, "you drive closer than that to cars on the highway." "Pull up.....WHACK.....ok, Paul," said Mona, "that's close enough."

Did all these awful drivers in my life prepare me

for the highways and byways in and around Sarasota, Florida, where I now spend my winters.

It's very scary out there, my friends.

Paws For The Comedienne

Only once in a person's life does a dog like Skeena come along.....hopefully. She was named after the scenic, meandering river in British Columbia, Canada. As an adult dog she weighed about seventy-five pounds, had flashing brown eyes that turned demoniac as soon as she put her ears back, and a coat so thick, a blanket could have been woven from the hair. Her face was that of a wolf, but with a perfect mask. She was a gorgeous Alaskan Malamute and we belonged to her.

Skeena was part of the family, and from my point of view, she was part of the family, we could do without. She felt the same way about me. To her, I was nowhere close to the top, in the chain of command, and thus, expendable. Paul, my husband, was first, she was second and I was somewhere down the list.

As a pup, she was totally unmanageable. Put a collar and lead on her, she sat down and would not move. She would not sit, stay, or come, if she did not want to, and a neighbor told us, that if we beat her into submission (which would never have entered our minds) we would no longer have a malamute, we would have a dog.

She was about five months old, when she experienced her first snowfall. We had been visiting Paul's parents and were planning on staying the night. The evening had been bone-chilling cold and by morning, there was a foot of snow on the ground. Skeena stepped out onto the balcony. She stopped, stared, and when realization hit, she put her nose into the snow and erupted. She flew off the balcony, all four legs splayed. She hit the pavement running from one side, of the lawn to the other. She raced down the side walk, ran across the road and back, jumping from snow pile to snow pile, with Paul and me in hot pursuit. We never came close to catching her. When we could no longer catch our breath, we went back to the balcony and discussed trading her in, on a Chihuahua. We now wished for some little animal that would quiver in these frigid climes and cross her paws until the snow melted, before going outside.

We waited, while Skeena ran the streets and we prayed that she would not meet a car head on. It took about forty-five minutes before she came tearing back, bounding up the stairs, and threw herself at Paul. He caught the quaking mass and carried her into the kitchen, where she bolted and hit the floor, with a thud. She drank a huge bowl of water, wolfed down her food and plopped herself on the rug in the corner. She lay there for hours, reliving the joy of the outdoors, moaning and twitching.

For the years she shared our lives, we trained her as best we could and just enjoyed her antics. We had an endless supply of stories to tell. She had a wicked sense of humor and she knew it, like the time she scared the hiker.

One week end, we took her walking on the Bruce Trail in Southern Ontario. Since there were only a few cars in the parking lot, we assumed there would be few people on the trail, so we let her off the lead. Although she was a large beast, she was gentle with people, and only groundhogs took the full brunt of her wrath. Skeena led the way up the trail and stopped at berry patches, to pluck off the fruit with her lips, while she waited for us to catch up. Close to the top, she vanished. We had no idea where she was, until we saw some wild-eyed young man, backing away from the bushes, shaking violently and mumbling “holy shit, holy shit”. As he continued backing up, getting closer to a deep crevasse, Skeena poked her head through the bushes, obviously for the second or third time. She knew she was scaring the hell out of the guy and she loved it. While he teetered on the edge, we spoke quietly, so he wouldn't panic and jump. " She's a dog," Paul said, "look at her collar". "Look at her collar! She's a dog!" he repeated a few more times. He calmed down slowly, but never took his eyes off her. Skeena lowered her head and appeared to be laughing and coughing at the same time.

One day we decided to test her loyalty. Trying to sound angry, I had my husband pinned against the wall, in our bedroom. I was yelling and slapping the wall with my hand, Skeena jumped on me, in an effort, to protect him. A few days later we reversed the order and Paul had me pinned to the wall. Skeena went between his legs and jumped on me, helping him pin me to the wall. I'm sure if it had been an intruder, instead of my husband, Skeena would have seen it as a golden opportunity to eliminate me from her life. A guard dog for me, she wasn't.

She loved the water. On one winter outing, she broke through the ice and was swimming around in a rather large hole. Paul managed to find some planking, laid it beside the hole and pulled her out, by the scruff of her neck. She ran around madly, shaking all the water off, until she was dry and we were soaked and then jumped in again, to finish the game she had started. Winter or summer, the water was a real treat to her; however, drizzle a bit of shampoo onto her back and she howled like a banshee. People around were sure she was suffering the tortures of the damned. What an actress.

Skeena would sit beside Paul's chair while we watched television some evenings. Occasionally she would poke her nose under his resting hand. Paul would pet her. A minute or so later, she would poke him again and he would pet her again. She waited and would poke him again. She did this until Paul became aggravated with her and would try to slough her off by looking at her and saying "WHAT". She backed off. She waited and poked him again. Paul would put his face closer and closer saying WHAT.....DO.....YOU.....WANT? When Paul became most annoyed and would be nose to nose with the dog, she would burp in his face. She would lower her head and expel air. She was laughing. No question about it. She was laughing.

Her evening treat, was a couple of hours, to roam our property and a jaunt into our woods. When we got tired of yelling for her, we turned on the popcorn machine. By the time the first kernel of corn hit the top of the machine, she was pawing at the door. Ice cream had the same effect, but it didn't make noise, so we resorted to popcorn; however, if that particular kernel missed the dabble of butter, it was spit back. If it got too late for popcorn, we would yell for her to come back. The later the hour, the harsher our voices became. When we were so angry, that she knew, if we caught her, we would kill her, she would shoot past us, run into her kennel, close the door and hide in her house. All we could do was lock the door behind her.

She knew exactly what she wanted and she accepted no less. She loved popcorn and ice cream and cold weather and playing frisbee with the plastic top of our large garbage can and burying one of each our boots and shoes in the snow, but mostly, she loved Paul.

They are together always.

Hey Buddy, Have You Seen My Wife?

Same as Paul's on the side, a little longer on top, was my standard answer to Sam, when he asked how I wanted my hair cut. Paul, my always impeccably dressed, husband, had neatly trimmed, blond hair on the sides and nothing on top.

It took a year or more of Sam the Barber, my next door neighbor, asking if he could cut my hair, before I let him touch my curly, salt and pepper gray, mop.

On one particular day, I was really looking forward to my day off, from work. My hair had grown a fraction too long and had gone wild, about a week before. I always looked forward to getting it cut. I like it short, as straight as I could get it and out of my eyes. I gave her the order, "short, please" and let my beautician go about her business. Janie, who worked at a salon close to my home, had cut my hair many times before, so I didn't give it a moment's thought and went back to reading.

I took a quick glance, while she was cutting the top, and when all appeared normal, I relaxed and turned the page of my book. With the next glance, my eyes bulged in disbelief. What the hell had she done! The top was shorter than I had ever seen it. Had I been a teenaged boy, it would have been called a brush cut. The one side she had cut, was so short, all the hairs were visible and standing straight out. No amount of brushing would make it lie flat and my only recourse, was to have her duplicate the side.

Oh, what the hell, I thought, resigning myself to the situation. No point in making a scene. There were no important functions in the near future, no family or business dinners coming up and my hair grows really quickly, I thought. I paid, tipped her , and left. I went home, busied myself with other projects and soon forgot about the disastrous hair cut.

My husband called around 5:00 P.M. "I'm glad your home, Hon," he said. "I locked my keys in the car." "If you bring my spare set, I'll buy dinner." "A deal," I said. "I'll meet you at King and Bay, southwest corner." "I'm leaving in five minutes."

I cursed and swore at the rush hour traffic, in downtown Toronto and was relieved when I saw Paul waiting patiently. He opened the passenger side door, looked at me and quipped "Hey Buddy, have you seen my wife?" "Shut up and get in, let's get out of here," I retorted. Upset with the traffic, I was not prepared for a discussion about my hair. "Besides," I reminded him "it's still longer than yours." "Touché," was his only remark.

The following morning, while unlocking the door to my wool shop, I poked my head into Sam's Barber Shop. He looked and pointed "and you paid for that," he said, hardly able to control his laughter. Three months later, Sam gave me my first hair cut.

That was over ten years ago. In 1989, I closed my wool store, to go traveling. In 1992, my husband Paul, died; however, twice a year, Sam still cuts my hair. In October, before I leave for Florida and in April, before I leave for parts unknown, I stop on the Danforth, in Toronto, for my hair cut and to talk with my friend.

I Was Not Supposed To Be Here Alone

Florida was to be our hideaway, from the torturous weather of the north. My husband, Paul and I, would winter in sunshine, playing golf, swimming, hiking, biking and volunteering. Perhaps we would spend a day or two working, each week, at something we enjoyed. I could teach knitting or a class in needlepoint and Paul could work at a golf course or help a carpenter, anything to work with his hands.

It had been a ten year old dream to semi-retire in Florida

We took six months finding the perfect hideaway and slowly, we moved in our belongings. We took the time to put everything in its place. We moved in and stayed two days. It was May and getting hot in Florida. We sealed the condo and left to go traveling. We went back to Canada to visit friends and family and then back to Europe.

Our dream turned to a nightmare. In the blink of an eye, my life went from riding high to the depths of widowhood. A heart attack, while jogging in a German campground, had taken my husband, in the prime of life.

Not only did I have to contend with widowhood, I had to do it in a place, with no family and only a few newly made friends, in Sarasota, Florida.

In the years that have passed, I discovered many things:

Happy or not, the years go by very quickly.
I can travel alone.
I hate staying home.
I love getting up at 5:00 A.M. and writing.
I make friends easily.
I think I've lost my kitchen.

I love camping and sightseeing and movies and plays and opera and dancing and television and golf, and after four long years, I tolerate Florida. I do not like it.

I Was Not Supposed To Be Here Alone.

The Lonesome Traveler

My stomach was in a knot and my head pounded and "never drive when angry" kept coming to mind. But what was I to do. I needed to remove myself from the situation or go berserk. I needed my family so "I drove angry".

The person I had rented my condominium to, had stopped payment, on the last month's rent. When I learned that my air conditioner had died one muggy, Floridian day and could not be repaired, I drove there from New Mexico to check it out. Since, I was told, that the tenant had moved, I went into the condo. He moved, his belongings did not.

My home was a mess. He had piled his furniture on top of mine and what couldn't be "piled on" he put on my unairconditioned lanai. His cat, which he had forgotten to mention, had used one of my kitchen drawers as a cat bed, or worse, and when I called my tenant at work, to tell him to get his things out of my home, he returned that evening, changed the lock and refused to leave until the lease was up.

With just a few articles of clothing, my toiletries and my credit cards, I left my neighbor's home around noon and headed north. I drove to Valdosta, Georgia, stopping only for gasoline.

Driving usually relaxes me and this was no exception, but I still did not feel well. I felt displaced, despondent and homeless - I would have to fight to get my home back.

Why had I rented to him in the first place? He was newly divorced, desperately needed a place to stay and I was leaving - these three elements, combined, would prove to be my downfall, I felt.

My choice for a motel room that night was a poor one. The room was spacious, clean and provided all amenities but it was well back in the motel lot and there were not many people around. I was nervous and didn't really want to drive to go out to dinner, but I did it anyway.

Dinner was tasteless, even though I had ordered my favorite, shrimp. It had been a long day of driving and now I was alone and agitated. I ate a bit and took the rest back to my room in the hope that I would nibble a bit.....I didn't. I slept fitfully, but I slept.

The next day was another long, drive day. I stopped twenty miles south of Lexington, Kentucky and made a better choice of hotel. I took an hour to close my eyes, letting the television set drone in the background and then a long, slow, relaxing bath, allowing the hot water to drain every bit of stress from my body, before dressing for dinner.

Dinner, at the Cracker Barrel Restaurant, was right across the parking lot and was crowded. Seeing all the people milling around, took my mind off my problems, for a while. I gave my name and the number in my party, to the waitress. There were many people ahead of me on the list, including a gentlemen who would be dining alone.

I shopped, I browsed, I handled each piece of merchandise and I waited. The longer I waited, the more agitated I became. I wanted to talk to someone.....anyone. I checked the list.

Perhaps the people, whose names were on the list, after my name, said they wanted smoking, but both the name ahead of mine and mine were skipped over. The gentlemen was approaching.

I screwed up my courage and said quickly "we both seem to be dining alone in the non-smoking section, would you care to share a table?" The change on his face was dramatic and immediate. His eyes glowed. He was as thrilled with the prospect of a dinner companion, as I was. We were chatting even before we arrived at our table.

"I'm heading south," he said. "I was visiting my daughter and grandchildren in Toledo, for a few days." "I miss them and it's so far from Atlanta." "I see them only a couple times a year now."

"I spend my winter in Florida," I confided, "but my family lives in Toronto." "I miss them, too, but I spend six months of the year traveling." "I have a condo in Sarasota."

"We live in a senior residence in Atlanta," he volunteered.

"We," I asked "your wife doesn't drive with you to see your children."

"No," he replied, a touch of sadness in his voice, "she has Alzheimer's and doesn't recognize anyone, anymore."

"I'm so sorry." "Must be terribly difficult to deal with, how long have you been married?" I asked.

"Fifty-one years."

"That's how old I am," I said, "fifty-one years." "A lot can happen in fifty-one years." "I have been a widow for three of those years."

"I'm sorry," he said, "I know that I shouldn't be telling you this, but I now have a lady friend." "I cannot tell my daughter, she wouldn't understand."

"I know it's lonely," I said, "and you have to take the joy, where you find it." "I'll find it again some day, I know."

"I know you will," he said, "you're a very pretty lady." "Where did you travel to, this year?" he asked, opening an entirely new theme to the conversation.

"I drove to Alaska," I said. "I cannot believe how much driving I will have done this summer, by the time I get back to my home." "If I get my home back," I said, almost under my breath.

"What do you mean," he asked, "if you ever get your home back?"

The conversation never stopped. The hour of sharing had changed my mood, my outlook, my entire day, in fact, and only at the end of the meal did we introduce ourselves. We thanked each other, as we said our good byes, in the parking lot and shook hands. We wished each other a safe journey and parted.

Would it be so difficult, particularly in areas of high travel, to have one table, with four or six chairs, set aside for people traveling alone, who would like to share conversation with other lonesome travelers?

Small Steps to Freedom

Chapter 1

"You don't have to do this, you know?" said my sister-in-law, Sandra. "You can have someone over there sell it for you." "You don't have to go back." "Do you really think Paul would want you to go through so much pain?" Sandra asked.

"Sandra," I replied, showing some annoyance, "what's going to happen to me that's going to be worse than has already happened?" "I must sell the van and I must make it mine before I do." "I must get my life back into some kind of order."

It had been almost a year since my husband, Paul, had died and the pain was still overwhelming most of the time. It was almost crippling. He had died so quickly. We had been traveling through Germany and camping in the van. He went jogging, had a heart attack and died in a stranger's car on the way to the hospital. His life and mine were over in minutes. How a person's life can go from riding high to the depths of despair, in a heartbeat, will always remain a mystery to me.

The only thing I knew, was that things had to be taken care of in order. If I never saw the van again and someone sold it for me, I felt my life would never get beyond wanting to see the van again. I would spend my life regretting not having handled things myself. I would regret not having found some treasure in the van, that belonged to Paul. I needed to do this. The sooner the pain was faced, the sooner I could live with it. Indeed, what could happen to me that would be worse than had already happened?

On the day of his death, June 26th, 1992 the last line of my diary read - My life is gone. I don't remember exactly when I wrote it, but how appropriate. Losing Paul had left a void in my life, the size of the Grand Canyon. My heart had shattered into so many pieces that even now, I know I will never be whole again. He was the joy and the fun in my life. He was my life.

I often wondered why people let so many years go by before they write about a loved one who has died. I now know why they wait so long. It is too painful, to put on paper. It becomes too real, if it is written down.

I had to return to England. I had to learn to drive the van, to sleep in it, to camp in it, to cook my meals in it.....to make it mine and to sell it.

My family and friends felt it was too early and would be too painful. In my heart, I knew they were right, but what was I to do? How could I let the home we had traveled in for two and a half years rust away, with no care. We had loved our little home on wheels, had loved the traveling and had loved being together, even after sixteen years of marriage.

* * * *

I landed at Gatwick Airport. Although being alone was new to me, England was not. I took the train to London from the airport and found my way to the main train terminal. Without too many problems, or asking too many people, I located the correct train and made my way to a friend's house in Otford, Kent, just south of London.

I had spoken to Amanda's husband several days earlier in Toronto, Canada so she was expecting me. She knew from my letters that I had hoped and planned on spending some time on an archaeological dig. Since a neighbor of hers was involved in the Archaeological Society in Kent, she arranged for me to be on the dig as soon as I arrived.

I did not have an opportunity to get over jet-lag. I arrived at the house mid-afternoon on June 25th, Amanda and I spent some time talking and catching up on each others lives, and the next day, I was digging. Since I was already exhausted from the all night flight, I did not have a spare moment to grief, any more or any less, on the 26th. The day just passed.

Thanks to the Webers, Bill and Amanda, my Canadian friends, several days passed. Every moment of every day, I stayed busy. I helped out with the cooking. I babysat. I did some ironing. I kept Amanda company and spent most of my day at the dig site, but once the lights went out at night, the tears came.

I knew the hospitality would not last forever. I would have to, at some point, acquire some courage and retrieve the van that had been stored in Barry, Wales, just south of Cardiff.

I had been in England about five days. The dig in Otford was over. Although, I did not sleep well that night and was plagued with bad dreams, I took the train to Cardiff the following day. I made my way, to the Barry docks and even before I saw the van, I could feel myself fighting back the tears. I forced myself not to look.

Randy Bassett, dark haired with a warm smile, was a very handsome man in his mid fifties and owner of the storage company. When not in use, the van had been stored there for about three years and although he did not know me well, he was aware of my circumstances.

We went to get the van together. I could feel the tears stinging my eyes and my throat starting to choke. The trembling starting in my belly, slowly consuming my body until I could not contain the sobs. Once at the van, under the pretext of a phone call, Randy left me alone for a while. By the time he returned, I had done my best to control myself.

It had been almost a year since I had seen or started it, but Randy assured me that we would get the van going and he would not leave me until it did.

It started a lot easier than I would have anticipated; however, this would be the easy part. I still had to drive it. I had never really been alone in it. I had never driven it more than a block or two and even then, my husband had been at my side.

It was an English van so the steering wheel was on the wrong side. I would be shifting with the wrong hand and I would be driving on the wrong side of the road. I had no idea how to get to Cardiff, from where I was. Even with Randy there beside me and knowing that he would help as best he could, I would soon be alone in the van and I numbed myself, so the terror I felt, would not show through.

I drove out of the compound and once back at his office, Randy called his service station to make sure they could take care of a tuneup. I called the insurance company and had full coverage reinstated. With the storage bill paid, and a round of good lucks from the staff, I left. Once behind the steering wheel and on the road, my stomach tied itself into an knot. What I really wanted to do was just stop the van on some side road and cry until I died. Somehow, I just kept driving.

The garage was a mile away and once there, the van was tested and certified, roadworthy, quickly. The mechanic was kind enough to do a major inspection, thanks to Randy, and made sure everything was really all right and working. He also took over an hour to wash the van. It had been left under a tree that had dropped resin all over it.

They were doing a thorough job on the washing and I was getting anxious. It was quite late in the afternoon, and I was desperate to be on the way. Driving the van would be difficult enough, I did not want to be driving it at night. It was still nine miles to Cardiff, and the roads were so narrow and winding.

"Please finish," my mind yelled, "why doesn't he shut up and finish the God damn washing and stop talking." I could feel myself beginning to panic and there was no one around to help. I forced myself to maintain control. I tried so desperately to calm down.

The people at the garage assured me that the route was well marked but the drive was slow. Each mile seemed to be a torturous eternity. I had to just keep driving. I concentrated on the road but nothing looked familiar. It was all so confusing and my mind was in such a turmoil. The signs said straight ahead to Cardiff - 7 miles..... 6 miles. Oh, my God, what happens if I get lost in Cardiff? Please let me just get there.....4 miles. Please, let me get there, I'll be ok....2 miles. "Please don't let me get lost," I prayed.

Once in Cardiff; however, the castle, which was my landmark, was evident from almost every street. I could suddenly hear myself breathing. I drove directly to the Castle, made my way around to the back and took one of the side streets, into the campground.

The office was closed. I drove straight in, pulled into one of the camping spots, stopped the van, turned off the key and dropped my head to the steering wheel. Clutching the steering wheel, the only source of strength I could hold, I broke down. Relief, anger, sick at heart, fatigue, perhaps all rolled into one, enveloped me. There I was, in an Welsh campground.....all alone.

My God, how was I going to manage, the thought screamed in my head. I had a three month, non-refundable, airline ticket. I don't know how long I cried. I just cried until I was empty.

Exhausted, I dried my face as best I could and went into the washroom to clean up a little. On the way back to the van, I stopped to talk with a couple who were sitting outside their camper. After a few pleasantries, I asked where I could find a grocery store, that might be open. Since it was almost six o'clock, I needed some little thing to eat and coffee for the morning. They directed me to a small, local grocery store, that I could get to, walking . I thanked them and left. I had to eat something, even though my stomach was still in a knot and my head was pounding.

I found the shop, picked up a couple of buns, tomatoes, cheese, butter, coffee and sugar and walked back to the van. Once the sandwich was made and I started eating, the tears returned and I could force myself to swallow only a few mouthfuls.

Becoming angry and frustrated with myself, again, I headed for the washroom. I composed myself as best I could, washed my face and ran a comb through my short cropped, prematurely gray, hair. The lack of sleep and the crying, had taken its toll. My eyes looked sunken and tired and I wished for some lipstick, so I would not look so pale, but, when I felt I looked fairly decent, I went visiting.

I knocked on the door where the folks had been kind enough to give me directions to the grocery store. She greeted me warmly and swung the door open wide. "Oh," she said, as I stepped inside, "are you alone?" Before I could control myself, the tears flooded out. Her arm immediately went around my shoulders protectively. "Come on in, have a cup of tea." "Get her a brandy," she motioned to her husband. I tried to apologize, but she just led me to the table and sat me down.

Through sobs, I recounted my story. They listened patiently, not commenting, just nodding their heads from time to time and whispering the occasional "oh dear" or "oh my". Slowly, I relaxed, letting the brandy take effect and I suddenly felt very grateful for people to talk to and to listen to me. The longer I talked, the calmer I became.

Gradually the subject changed and we talked well into the night. With the help of another visiting friend, the conversation became humorous. My crying jag was over for the evening and for the moment, it felt all right. The brandy helped, as did the laughter.

Nia, the other guest, who had been kind enough to listen to my story, lived close by and invited us all to brunch in the morning. I knew that I had many chores to take care of the next day, but brunch would be a welcomed way to start the day.

Small Steps to Freedom

Chapter 2

Thanks to the help of my new found friends, brandy included, I managed to sleep through some of the night, without too much tossing and turning.

After a relaxing brunch, that morning, and a walk through Nia's small English garden, we all said goodbye. Nia went back to work and my friends went back to the campground.

The rest of that morning, I spent walking through Cardiff, taking care of many necessary items of personal business.

I got the van road taxed (licensed). I closed my bank account at Barclay's Bank and removed the last of my British Sterling from an account, that had stayed intact, from the previous year. I found the insurance company and paid for my vehicle insurance. Paying that bill took care of most of the money, that I had left, in my British account. The fact that I was a foreigner, and a woman, made highway robbery legal, where insurance was concerned.

Much of the afternoon was spent at the Archaeological Society of Cardiff. The Archaeological Society had an office in the museum, so while I waited, I visited the museum. I was hoping to find a dig, that I could participate in, close to Cardiff.

After trudging from office to office and wandering the museum for hours, I learned they did not need any volunteers, at any of the dig sites. Although very disappointed and close to tears, I refused to despair. "I am a survivor," I thought, "I'll get through this."

That evening, I called friends in Temple Cloud, England, twelve miles south of Bristol.

Although my friends, Bob and Joan Higgins, were not at home, the people they shared the house with, Bonnie and Glenn Webster, sounded like they expected my call. Bonnie said she, and her husband, would welcome me, when I arrived, if the Higgins were not at home.

I was most grateful for a friendly voice; however, I would now have to drive the van more than seventy-five miles. I had driven it less than ten miles so far and was not the least bit comfortable behind the wheel.

Again, panic started to set in and my mind wandered in a hundred directions. I had no idea where the highways were or how to get out of Cardiff. I would have to read a map while driving and I would have to find my way through the heart of Bristol, a major sized city. I would be driving on the wrong side of the road, sitting on the wrong side of the van, shifting with the wrong hand AND in a depressed state of mind.

This trip was total lunacy and I was just beginning to realize it. I could suddenly hear my heart pounding and I was taking short gasping breaths. Hyperventilating had not been unusual for me in the past year. My shoulders slumped as I walked back to my camper.

I did not sleep well again, and this night, two chairs and a table came crashing down from an overhead rack, narrowly missing my head. "I will have to start selling things off," I thought in the wee hours of the morning. The table, chairs, a bicycle rack, radio, golf clubs and in the end, when I felt that the van was mine, and not ours, the van, would have to be sold.

I knew that it was too early to think about; but, I would not be happy traveling by myself and I did not want anyone else in the van, that I shared with my wonderful husband. I tried pushing all those thoughts to the back of my mind. A rock and a hard place, Catch-22, shit or go blind - all my favorite expressions popped into my mind.

Besides, I thought, the van should be used, not stored for months at a time, sitting idle and rusting away.

My new friends, and next door neighbors at the campground, had left before I awoke on that second morning. They had written out directions for me, on getting out of Cardiff. I had asked their help, after my telephone call to Temple Cloud, the evening before and they had been happy to oblige.

I screwed up my courage and left the campground around mid-morning, hoping that I had missed the early traffic jams. With every mile of driving, I gained a little confidence. The city roads were clearly marked with directions for getting to the highway. I was grateful for the written direction; but I hadn't really needed them.

I actually relaxed a bit driving the motorway and released the death grip, I had on the steering wheel. Slowly and carefully I made my way through Bristol and found the A37 heading south. I did not have to look for highway signs, since the large, white, route numbers were painted on the road. There was no way I could miss them. It was mid-afternoon when I arrived in Bristol and there was not much traffic on the road. Besides, I had highlighted the route on my map in yellow, while still in Cardiff, so it was easier to follow.

Bob and Joan were shocked when I called from a variety shop in Temple Cloud. They had been willing to come get me, as far away as Bristol, if it became necessary. Over the telephone, they directed me to the farm, which was one turnoff, from the main road and they were outside, standing on the street, waiting to cheer me, when I arrived. I could not have been more proud, if I had skyrocketed, myself to the moon.

I soon discovered, that although Bonnie had

greeted me warmly on the phone, the evening before, she had no idea who I was, where I had come from or how I had met the Higgins. She simply greeted everyone the same way.

"My husband and I, met Bob and Joan, while camping at the boat club in Menton, France, two years ago," I explained. " We became friends for the few days that we camped together and exchanged addresses." "While Joan was in Canada two weeks ago," I said, "we spent the day touring in downtown Toronto and now, here I am, on her doorstep."

While recounting my story, Joan, Bonnie and I did short work, on a large bottle of wine and it was the first time I relaxed since arriving in Britain.

I was welcome to stay with them for as long as I wanted, everyone in both families told me, and I relaxed for the few days, that I did stay. It did not take long; however, before I became edgy. I felt I had to move on.

Something happens to people "on a mission," I thought. I had no idea what I was looking for. I certainly had no idea, what I would find. I just had to fill a tiny portion of the tremendous emptiness that had been left in my life. I felt I had to keep going.

For the week that I spent in the Bristol area, I was wined and dined and entertained like royalty. The Higgins, who were both retired, and in their sixties, loved having company. They loved touring, and since they lived in a beautiful area, with lots of history, guests gave them a chance to see it all again.

We visited Cheddar Gorge and Wokey Hole, famous for their caverns. We had lunch on the grounds of the Wells Cathedral. We spent a day in Bath and other days touring the countryside, in their motorhome. Every restless moment I had, they filled with interesting friends and relatives, fascinating places and love.

Bob took one afternoon to check and change the oil, check the radiator and inspect all the belts and hoses in my van and we took the van out for a ride to make sure it was running properly.

The Higgins could not have done more. They did everything to assure me that one day my life would be back to something close to normal and tolerable, and even without a husband, we were all friends and helpmates. In quiet moments, Joan listened and cried with me.

Several weeks before leaving Canada, I had written to friends, Curt and Heidi Sampson, who owned an exotic, plant nursery, near Colchester. I called Heidi while I was with the Higgins and told her of my plans to head her way and "could you put me to work for a while?" I asked.

"There is always lots and lots of work to do, so come ahead when you can," she said.

With each accomplishment, I felt one step closer to freedom. My journey was made in a series of small steps.

I left the Higgins' place, knowing that I could return at anytime. It was an exhilarating feeling, knowing that I could try it on my own, and if I failed, a safety net would be there to catch me. I felt so grateful for these friends, and one morning, feeling a little braver than usual, I got behind the wheel of the van and got back on the road.

In between Bristol and Colchester, is Otford. I stopped for a day or two, to visit with my friends from Canada, who had arranged my first archaeological dig. Amanda did not seem to mind when I showed up. She was thrilled with the fact that I would do all the cooking. I found myself inventing all kinds of things in the kitchen and both she, and her husband, loved it. Her children, on the other hand, looked upon me as very weird and told me so, often. I would arrive at odd times, move in and stay for a while, and then be gone.

Sometimes I would leave before the children awoke in the morning. Also, I had the same strange accent as their mummy and daddy, so I always peeked their curiosity. This time I stayed in Otford, only a day or so, before driving out to Colchester.

What surprised me most, was the way I made my way around England. The route numbers were very clearly marked. I had no trouble maneuvering through the narrow streets, although I did drive very slowly. At times the mirrors on the van, touched bushes on both sides of the street. But I made it.

After all, I repeated to myself more often than I cared to admit, I am a survivor.

Small Steps to Freedom

Chapter 3

How could I have gotten myself into this mess? My depression hit a new low.

I was really pleased when I arrived in Dedham, near Colchester, and got a wonderfully, warm reception from my friends, Curt and Heidi. I knew, also, that there would be plenty of work for me to do and I could keep busy, for as long as I wanted.

Paul and I had met Curt, in the first year of our travels. Curt was a bearded, giant of a man, wearing size fifteen shoe, and he was vacationing, in the Canary Islands. He was there alone because Heidi had gone to visit family in Austria. He wasn't enjoying his vacation, until we came along and invited him to join us, in seeing some of the sights.

"You'll have to come to England to meet my Heidi," he would say often, and on our return trip to England, we did meet her. She was just as Curt had described.....petite, blond, very energetic and lots of fun. She was a writer of children's books, gourmet cook, wholistic medicine healer, and a bit of the devil, all rolled into one.

I was thrilled when she had told me to come to Dedham and that there would be lots of work for me to do. Physical labor always seemed to help control my mental pain. If I wore myself down physically, I thought, I wouldn't think too much. Since I never slept well, I looked forward to exhaustion.

By the second day, I was selling plants at a flower show, at the local county fair. It would have been more interesting had been busier; but, it was a start. The following day I was propagating plants. That job required shoving and lifting heavy boxes.

Heidi kept me company some of the time and

at other times, had lots of work, of her own, to do. The physical labor eased my mind, but the work was too taxing on an untrained body. Within three days, I had done such heavy, constant, labor that I pulled my back out and could no longer move very well.

With every move, I was in agony and took a day off to sit with pillows, propping my back. I used pain killers, to relieve the soreness, while I read and watched television. For that one day the work continued without me.

While I was healing, Heidi showed me how to use the computer. We played some computer games, for an hour, and then she put me to work. I learned to do some invoicing and when that was done, I put new customer's names and addresses into the system.

When we were alone, in the office, Heidi confided her problems to me. I was already aware of the underlying tension that surrounded the home life and I did not want to get involved. She talked constantly about selling the business and the house and getting out; while Curt, when we were all together, talked about his plants and his love for them. He loved the heavy labor and the outdoors, but knew nothing about the business end.

Heidi took care of all the book work, all the computer work, much of the heavy labor, all of the house work, and all of the cooking. Her body was having trouble coping with everything. Arthritis was taking its toll on her. She talked constantly of selling out from under him. I'm sure he suspected; but, he never let on. The tension was horrible.

One day, after a morning of work, Heidi and I were playing games on the computer. Curt pushed the door open, and, in a voice that would wake the dead, boomed "LUNCH". No prelude, no niceties, just LUNCH. I thought he was kidding, but his voice scared the hell out of me. Looking at her watch, Heidi said that it was past his lunch time and that lunch should be on the table. Lunch was to be served at 1:00 P.M.. It was now 1:03 P.M.

After the LUNCH incident, my mood turned black. I knew that I had to get away. I knew, also, that I had no idea where I would be going. I still had some friends that I wanted to visit; but, I felt I could not leave this place without Heidi knowing "why". Plus, I had promised Heidi that I would work the Peterborough Show and Fair. I slumped into a real depression, and had no one to talk to, about it. Heidi saw the change in me immediately and she did her best to help.

We didn't talk much but she gave me a variety of work to do that was not too taxing on my back. I typed labels. I stuffed envelopes. I deposited cheques. We spent a day at the health club, doing exercises and swimming and we talked about the upcoming county fair that we would be attending. The time passed.

We drove to the Peterborough Show and Fair. Heidi drove with me and Curt took one of his employees, and drove a truck, pulling a trailer with all the plants. After we set up the display, Heidi and I spent three days working at the Peterborough Fair by ourselves. Curt went off to exhibit and sell at another flower show in London.

It was amazing how relaxed everything got when the Lord and Master of the house was not around. We could work, talk, enjoy the customers and have coffee, all the while, making money. We ate when we were hungry.

Since Heidi had been going to this Show and Fair for many years, most of the customers that came around, knew of the Pegasus Center. One customer, invited us back to their home for dinner. After the show closed that night, the gentleman, Bob Thomas, came to pick us up. That evening there was lots of talk, lots of wine, lots of fun and a tour of their beautiful garden. Most of the exotic plants, at their home, had been purchased at Pegasus Center.

The next night we drove back to the Center in the dark. Curt and his employee had driven out to the show to help us pack up and go. Tension returned.

Jimmie drove with me and I was grateful to have the company. Since I would not have been able to follow Curt, in the dark, I was relieved to have someone with me, who knew the way.

We stopped for dinner about half way through our trip. Once back at the house, however, things became unbearable again. It was not what they were saying.....it was what they weren't saying. Everything was underlying and I did not want to be around when it exploded. I knew that it would.

I tried to keep my distance, but it did not work. While in Pegasus, I wrote some letters back to my friends and family, in Canada, and they all worried about me, for weeks. The depression poured out of my heart right onto the paper and I couldn't stop it. There was no one at the nursery that I could talk to and it was killing me. I knew I had to get away.

After I had been at Pegasus Center over two weeks, I called Amanda, my Canadian friend living in Otford, to ask if the archaeological dig had started in Sevenoaks. I felt the dig would be a perfect reason to leave. Amanda answered, "no, not yet. Are you all right?"

"I'll be ok," I replied. Without a word of explanation, just the sound of my voice, Amanda knew that I was not all right. I got off the phone. I decided that if I did not make the break, I would lose my sanity. I called Helen and Barry Nixon, living only thirty miles away, in Creeting St. Mary.

When Helen extended an open invitation, I stayed in Colchester one more day and vowed that I would never put myself in such an uncomfortable position again. I didn't have to say too much to

Heidi. She knew. The tension was no less for her.....only more familiar.

We said our goodbyes the following morning, knowing we would probably never see each other again.

Small Steps to Freedom

Chapter 4

After the hell I had experienced at Pegasus Center, Creeting St. Mary was such a treat. Paul and I had met Barry and Helen camping, on the Costa Del Sol, in Spain. They had been part of a large group, that had befriended us.

These were warm and welcoming people whose playful bickering was from a long standing and loving marriage. They were absolutely shocked to hear about the death of Paul, and even more shocked, at what I was doing, traveling around by myself.

I tried putting the events of the last few weeks behind me, so I could enjoy my visit with Barry and Helen. I spent my days helping out with the gardening and trimming hedges, going out for pub lunches, visiting Stolen Gardens and one afternoon was spent visiting Great Yarmouth, home of one of the largest motorhome dealerships in England. Since we were all motorhomers, this was a real event and although it was only a couple of hours drive, we turned it into a whole day's affair, picnic lunch and all.

While going through Ipswich, I found myself short of cash and used my new bank card for the first time. The ATM machine spit money back at me so fast, I hardly had time to get my hands under it. This machine wanted my secret access code and the amount. It did not care what account the money came from. I now felt a little more secure, knowing my traveling money, was close at hand.

That afternoon, my friend Helen, issued a challenge. She took me to the travel section of her favorite book store and told me she expected to see my name amongst the authors within five years.

This was a real challenge because I was neither writing at the time, nor had I ever written.

She seemed so proud of my accomplishments and she was sure that my spunk would lead to a different type of life.....and a good one.

The three days went by very quickly, with only one incident, that damn near drove me over the edge of sanity.

The night before I left, while watching television, I spotted a spider on the wall. A "spider" was not the word for it. When this monstrosity started walking, I could feel the vibration where I sat. It not only had long, thick legs, it had a huge body. I was glued to the sight of the thing. I could not yell, I could only point, wild-eyed and frantic. Helen followed my gaze, and when her eyes caught a glimpse of it, she screamed for Barry.

Helen, I'm sure, screamed, just to humor me. I was terrified. Except for seeing tarantulas behind glass, inside an aquarium at the pet shop, I had never seen anything so big.

Barry came, looked, and without a word, went back into the kitchen. He returned, quickly, with a jar and a newspaper in hand. He gently ushered the spider into the jar, covered the mouth of the jar with the newspaper and left the house. He was gone so long that when he returned, Helen asked, sarcastically "what did you do, take it to a pub for a drink?" "Where the hell did you go?"

In his usual soft-spoken manner, Barry explained that spiders have a homing device and if released too close to the house, they will return, instantly. "I took it out to the orchard and put it in a tree," he explained.

"Wonderful," I said, "a homing device." With dreams of the spider, hanging by a fragile web descending from the ceiling, I hardly slept that night; however, over breakfast, we talked and said our goodbyes. I assured them I would return, before going back to Canada. It had been these few days that renewed my faith in myself.

Each time I got behind the steering wheel of my motorhome, I felt like a pioneer. I was becoming more and more used to the van; however, up to this point, I really had not spent much time sleeping or camping in it.

Every time I felt that I was letting my friends do too much for me, I was reminded of Sister Jan DeVita, head of a bereavement group, that I had attended, in Toronto, Canada, who told me "If anyone wants to help you, let them. You will have time to repay them, or someone else, at a later date." I let her wise words guide me.

Norwich was my next conquest, with Deanna and Don Hunter, whom Paul and I had met in Athens, Greece, as my benefactors. As a group, we had spent, on and off, several months together. They had heard about Paul from our mutual friends in the United States and I knew that they wanted to see me. When I called them from Creeting St. Mary, they had given me directions to get to Norwich. I knew their address because I had written to them on a number of occasions, but they, too, were shocked when I knocked on their door. They were sure they would have to come retrieve me from some alleyway in Norwich; however, British maps are very precise and even the tiniest of roads, are marked with street names.

The yakking started even before the tea was made and we wiled away the afternoon and a good part of the evening. Even though they had a tiny apartment, I was told that the living room, with the sleeper sofa, was all mine for as long as I wanted to stay.

As of the next day, they were both on vacation. Their one vacation chore was to repaint their bedroom with a paint that would inhibit mold. It was the same problem that many English homes and apartments had -- the place was damp. "I'll stay," I said, "only if I can help." With the three of us working, we would have time to work and do some sightseeing, as well. They agreed.

The first day was spent stripping the existing wallpaper. By the end of that day Deanna and Don were at each other's throat, so Don was vanquished to rustproofing my van, while I helped Deanna. The jobs went very smoothly after that. We worked and talked and ate and cried for about five days, stopping only for meals and nightfall. All went well. I loved working with them, we could see results of the painting in the bedroom and the rustproofing on my van, quickly, and I paid for dinners out, so everyone was pleased.

While watching television one evening, we learned that an archaeological dig was underway and objects, of major importance, were found, in Scole, thirteen miles away. The following morning I went to the museum in Norwich to volunteer my services at the dig. I filled out an application and set about waiting......and waiting.....and waiting.

Almost two weeks passed. Deanna went back to work. Don had finished working on my van. Since his vacation was almost over, and I would soon be spending my days alone, I asked him if he wanted to take a ride out to Scole. The next morning, after breakfast, we drove there. We had no trouble finding the dig site, it was enormous.

I had nothing to lose. I asked to speak to the person in charge of volunteers and was immediately introduced to Alicia Landis. "Do you need any volunteers?" I asked. She answered with "when did you have your last tetanus shot?" I gave her the date as September, 1989 and she asked that I come in the next day and go to work. So much for sitting glued to the phone, for the museum to call, I thought.

I arranged to stay at the campground that was

located next to the dig site. I paid for camping for the following day. Don and I drove back to Norwich very lighthearted.

We celebrated that night, with wine. I was to return to Norwich for the weekends. Deanna did not want me to spend the days not working, in the campground, by myself. Their couch would be available for as long as I was in the area. "Besides," said Don, "we want to hear, first hand, what's going on at the dig." "We want the news before the telly," he grinned.

Small Steps to Freedom

Chapter 5

The thirteen mile drive, to the dig site, was exhilarating and I arrived before the crew. Three mini vans appeared suddenly and, in no time at all, the place was alive and active. Crew members picked up their assignments and when I approached Alicia Landis, she asked if I wouldn't mind waiting, until after the briefing. I made myself a pot of tea and relaxed in my van.

Once everyone was at work, it did not take Alicia long to find an assignment for me. I sat with seven other volunteers, all of whom had arrived after the briefing. Everyone introduced themselves, but, only when we took a break, did we chat and even then, it was mostly about the dig.

The first day at the dig, was also my first night in the campground, alone. I busied myself with dinner and had a good book to read.

It did not work. After dinner, knowing that I had all evening to myself, I became depressed. I walked through the campground, studying the few camping vans, that were there. One camper was the exact size that I had been looking at while in Great Yarmouth, at the motorhome dealership. Since it was around dinner time, I did not disturb them.

Later that evening; however, when a man left the camper, carrying the dinner dishes, I knocked on the door. The lady of the home, answered. With whatever smile I could muster, I explained that I had been looking at this exact camper and, I asked, "how do you liked this sized van?" She promptly invited me in and gave me the cook's tour.

I was ready to leave when the husband returned. He opened the door, saw me standing there, and said, "how wonderful, we have a guest, let's have tea." The evening passed most pleasantly. Their travels had been nowhere near as extensive as mine, and they were fascinated with stories about the dig. I touched only briefly on why I was traveling alone and then changed the subject.

Long past bedtime, flashlight in hand, they both walked me back to my camper and made sure that all was well before they left me. Their camper was gone before I went to work, the next morning.

The following night, a similar incident occurred. After dinner, while washing up my dishes, I chatted with a young woman, in the ladies room. She was delighted with the fact that it was so quiet in the campground.

I, of course, felt differently and told her so. "Since I'm alone," I explained, "I wish there were more people around." I wasn't back in my camper longer than two minutes, when there was a knock at the door.

"If you don't want to be by yourself," said the young woman, "please join us in our tent." "We have two children, and they are asleep," she said, "so we can't leave."

I needed no more coaxing. I put on my sneakers and was lacing them up, before she even finished the sentence. I picked up a bottle of wine from a storage area under the stove, grabbed my sweatshirt, and was off.

The situation I forced on myself, would have been intolerable, had it not been for the wonderful people, many of whose names I have forgotten or never knew, that I met along the way.

The days passed quickly at the dig, even though none of the jobs, seemed terribly interesting. All the work done was slow and meticulous, but there was an unmistakable camaraderie amongst all the people -- regular staff and volunteers.

Everyone was there for a cause, whether it

was a job for money, or a chance to be part of uncovering ancient history or, as in my case, just to be participating in life.

Evenings in the campground passed almost as quickly. From time to time, I was invited to the home of a volunteer, to have dinner with them and their family. I never spent one evening alone and on weekends, I returned to my friends in Norwich.

When the need for volunteers diminished, I left and went to visit my friends in Creeting St. Mary. They were delighted that I had decided to follow them, to Stoneleigh, for a camping festival.

Small Steps to Freedom

Chapter 6

The festival at Stoneleigh was healing and profitable. I did my camping with approximately four hundred other campers. There were parties to attend. There were lunches to enjoy. There were people to meet. There were people I had met years earlier, while camping in Spain, with my husband.

I took the opportunity, with so many campers around, to sell off my excess -- the radio, golf clubs, table and chairs. I put a sign in the window to sell the van. People seemed interested and asked a lot of questions; but, in the end, there were no buyers.

From Stoneleigh, I bade farewell to Barry and Helen Nixon, and once again, made my way back to Otford, to visit my Canadian friends. I was delighted to find several letters waiting for me, when I arrived. One was a birthday party invitation from my friend, Margaret James.

Paul and I had met Margaret and her husband, Dan, in France. They were both in their late sixties, and newlyweds. Over the years, we maintained a close friendship. I called Margaret's son, Neil, immediately, to let him know, that I would be there "with bells on".

Margaret was Welsh, and would be turning 70. She was as charming, as warm, as entertaining a woman, as Paul and I, had ever met. Dan was an American, from California, but we loved him, in spite of that flaw. I would not have missed her party and a chance to see them both again, under any circumstances. The party would take place in three weeks and I would busy myself until then.

I stayed in Otford awhile, helping Amanda. She was six months pregnant and facing food and cooking and caring for two very active boys was becoming a problem. I stayed and cooked. During the day, however, I had an opportunity to work on one more archaeological dig. I drove to Sevenoaks and signed up as a volunteer. Again, the time went quickly.

From Otford I drove to Cardiff. The party was held at the Barry Hotel, in Barry, Wales, about ten miles south of Cardiff. People came, from all over England and Wales, for the party. The Hotel gave us a special rate. It was cheaper staying at the hotel, than it would have been, in the campground.

It had been just over a year since I had seen them and because Dan had seen me in my camping gear only, he didn't recognized me. Seeing Margaret and Dan was one of the highlights of the trip. We laughed, and we cried, together.

Since Barry was a small seacoast village, the birthday party was the talk of the town. This part of Wales had never been known for its elegance. The champagne flowed and, if it was put into my glass, not a drop was wasted. We danced until the wee hours of the morning. I knew many of the people, at the party, since we had all wintered together in Spain, for a couple of years and everyone seemed to want to dance with the foreign lady.

The party continued the next morning with a champagne breakfast. The festivities lasted three days. I stayed a day or so after all the other guests left and Margaret and I, did a lot of talking. Everything said, we kissed goodbye and left, heading in different directions.

I drove back to Temple Cloud and stayed two weeks. I advertised the van, in the local Buy and Sell Magazine, hoping to sell it.

The Higgins and the Websters were amazed at my stories and my travels. I had been in England almost three months. I had traveled. I had camped. I had worked on archaeological digs. I had done all the things, I said I was going to do.

"When you arrived," said Bonnie, "you tried to sound so brave, and everything you said, was said through a voice, that was so shaky, we all knew, you were terrified." "We worried about you every day, that you were gone." " You really are brave now," she said.

They were right. I had done it. I had returned to them in three months a changed, person. Some of my confidence had returned.

In the end, I needed more than two weeks to sell the van. I put it back into storage, awaiting another trip. I knew that my traveling days were not over.

In fact, they were just beginning.

Digging Up Dirt

Chapter 1

Mona: You really don't have to do this, you know? reminded my sister, Mona.

Joei: Mona, I don't care if they hand me a shovel and tell me to "dig down for the next twelve layers."

Mona: That's the problem, they'll give you a teaspoon and tell you to dig the twelve layers. Then someone will come along with a paint brush and, with one sweep, will claim the glory.

Joei: Mona, do your friends still ask about me and how I'm doing?

Mona: All the time. They never heard such a sad story. It is everyone's greatest fear that something will happen on a vacation, when you're so far from home, but to be alone in a campground.....yes, they still ask how you're doing.

Joei: The first time someone asks how I'm doing and you say "not too well, she's really depressed," they'll wait about a month and ask again. The second time you say "she's not doing well," they might ask again. The third time, not only will they not ask, how I'm doing, they will avoid you, like the plague, because they don't want to know.

Mona: I understand what you're saying, but what's your point?

Joei: The next time your friends ask how I'm doing, you tell them that your sister is on an archaeological dig, in England, and they will hound you for information. They will want to know every minute detail. I don't care if it is boring. This is something Paul and I wanted and planned on doing together. Besides, just think of how this is going to look on my resume of life.

Mona: You're right, you know. I love you and be careful.

Joei: I will be careful, I promise. I love you too and I'll write you, all the time, so you won't have to worry about where I am.

This conversation took place two days before I left for England, in the summer of 1993, armed only with a list of Archaeological Societies, in the various counties, of England and Wales. I had sent off a few letters and hoped that some good news would be waiting for me when I arrived at a friends' house, Bill and Amanda Weber, in Otford, Kent, England, just south of London.

I arrived, suitcase over my shoulder, on the 25th of June. Just inside the door, before Amanda even stopped to hug me, she handed me a small package addressed, from the Archaeological Society of the United Kingdom. My fingers couldn't work fast enough, so Amanda slashed the package, with a sharp kitchen knife. Unfortunately the parcel contained the exact information that I had acquired in Canada, just names and addresses. Nothing that even indicated they would welcome hearing from me. Nothing at all.

After spending an hour or so, catching up on the news, with Amanda, she calmly announced that her next door neighbors, were involved in the Archaeological Society of Kent. Also, as calmly as before, Amanda said there was a small dig, going on in Otford, and she had signed me up to work with them.

The neighbors, Clive and Liza Warden, would be picking me up at 8:00 A.M. the following morning.

Thus started my summer of 1993.

Digging Up Dirt

Chapter 2

I was picked up, the following morning, by the Warden's and on the two mile drive, to the dig site, the reason for the "dig" was explained.

"When any outside work is being planned, the Archaeological Society in that area, is made aware, and tries to determine if anything of archaeological value is about to be covered up," I was told by Liza. "The Lassiter Family is planning on putting a tennis court in their back yard," Liza explained. "Their house, gardens and adjoining lands were once been part of the twelfth century Otford Palace. That palace is now in ruins within sight of their home," Clive added. "Test holes were dug and unearthed what seemed to be the stone floor of a blacksmith's shop, so the dig continues" Liza went on to explain. "The Archaeological Society doesn't mind something being covered up, as long as they know what it is," Clive continued.

By the time I arrived, most of the floor area had been cleaned away. The perfectly patterned out floor, sat in a twelve foot by twelve foot by one and one half foot deep, pit.

Using the trowel, as I was shown, I scraped away layer by layer around the floor. Working in conjunction with other members of the team, I uncovered nails and other bits of metal, that would later be identified as "probably" pertaining to a blacksmith shop. Several plastic bags were used to hold the bits and pieces, that were found in the different areas, of the dig site. Each bag was labeled with a number.

The day ended mid-afternoon and I was pleased. Working had helped me ease my way through jet lag, and being with several new people, whose interest was strictly archaeological, my focus was taken away from the fact, that it had been exactly one year, since my husband died.

For the next four days, I stayed focused on the dig. The evenings were spent with the Warden's, cleaning the artifacts. Buckets of cold water were used to remove outside debris, and a toothbrush was used, to scrape the artifacts clean. The articles were then numbered and rebagged. The numbers indicated where the dig took place and where, in the dig site, each artifact was found.

The days were spent doing manual labor at the dig site. The twelve foot by twelve foot area was cleaned with a brush, leveled and measured. Pictures were taken from every angle, along with pictures of the people working (that might have been done for my benefit). A pencil sketch drawing of the floor was made, making sure each stone was represented, then each stone was removed, to see what lay underneath, and then replaced, exactly as found.

When nothing more of significance was found, the Warden's wrote up a report, a shovelful of earth was put back in the hole and I determined, that my secondary reason for being in England, had commenced on a very positive note.

When I returned to Otford two weeks later, the Lassiter's had a brand new tennis court, in their back yard.

The second of my three digs, was the biggest and most exciting dig, going on in England in 1993.

Digging Up Dirt

Chapter 3

I had been staying with friends, in Norwich, on England's east coast, when the evening news, on television, aired the report of a fabulous find. The find was associated with a dig that was going on in, and around Diss, where an east/west and a north/south bypass, had been planned. Two Archaeological Societies were involved. Norfolk was working on one side of the River Waveney, while the Archaeological Society of Suffolk, worked on the south side. They had unearthed, for the first time, whole giant pots, unfired, that had been put in the peat in or around the year 300 A.D. and forgotten. This was a magnificent find, archaeologically speaking, and it certainly fired my interest.

Since my friends were on vacation, we walked to the museum in Norwich. That morning I filled out an application to volunteer, and waited by the phone. By the end of the following week, Deanna had returned to work, and Don would be going back to work in a couple of days. I had not heard from the museum and decided to take the bull by the horns. "Don," I asked, "want to take a drive and see if we can find the dig site?" "Sure, love it," he responded, "we'll take a drive out tomorrow, after breakfast."

We had no trouble finding the dig site. It was huge. Don and I took some time to walk the perimeter, to see what was happening. Many people were working in the pit, some with shovels, standing ankle deep in water, some on their hands and knees with a trowel, and some with brushes.

I asked to speak to the person in charge of volunteers and was ushered into the caravan office of Alicia Landis. Alicia was young, pretty, efficient and didn't mince words. I asked if she needed any volunteers? She asked when I had had my last tetanus shot? I told her September, 1989. She told me to come in the next day at 9:00 A.M. This, was after spending close to two weeks, waiting by the phone, for the museum to call.

Next to the archaeological site, was a campground. Don and I went to check out the facilities. It could not have been handier. I paid for one day of camping, so they would hold a spot, and told the manager, I would return the following day.

We celebrated that night with a lovely homemade pasta dinner and a special bottle of Bordeaux wine, from France. Although I would be working at the dig for a while, and I assured my friends, that, with so many people around, I would be fine, both Deanna and Don insisted that I come back to Norwich, for the weekend. Don was concerned that there were not many people in the campground. My friends did not want me there alone or uncomfortable, at any time. I agreed to return to their home for the weekend and thanked them for their concern.

Most of the paid personnel, working the archaeological site, were from Norwich and vicinity. A few of the volunteers lived in Diss and the surrounding area. The full-time employees were all picked up by minibus and shuttled to the dig site. That made sure they all got there and on time. When everyone arrived, coffee and tea was prepared and they had a morning briefing. Around 10:00 A.M. all work started.

I would love to be able to tell you that the job was fantastically exciting; however, my creative writing skills will never be, that creative. I now know how those tiny numbers, done with a nib and India ink, got onto each piece of everything.

"Each piece, no matter how small, needs a number," said Alicia. "You'll find the number on a piece of paper inside each bag." "The number," Alicia explained, "consists of the dig (107), the location of the dig (SC) Scole, and the exact spot the item was found, since the entire area was marked off in a grid."

I applied those numbers, for many hours, each day and when my back went out, from hunching over the desk, Alicia put me to work washing and toothbrushing the artifacts.

You could see that even the archaeologists did not have too interesting a task. On their hands and knees with a trowel they were uncovering layer by layer; however, when something of significance was uncovered or about to be uncovered, everyone was included. Someone usually made a special trip to the office to get the volunteers. We were rushed down to the spot to see a body, one with the brain still intact, or a large piece of pottery, waiting to be fired, or in one instance, a double casket, with the body of a child in it. Since children were never buried in caskets, and this was a double caskets, it was assumed, this was a special child. It was later determined that it may not have been a child, but an adult that had been buried in the fetal position. The excitement was in just being there and I loved it, as did many other volunteers.

When it was time for me to be on my way, the good byes were short, but I was told that there would always be room for me on any one of their digs.

On my last day in Scole, I was presented with a shard of Samien pottery, that had been found outside the dig area, and had remained intact from the year 300 A.D. I, however, managed to break it, several months later, on my return flight to Canada.

Digging Up Dirt

Chapter 4

Before the summer was over, I was to participate in one more dig. This dig was not as small as the first, nor as impressive as the second; but, now I could talk about my previous experience as a volunteer, and managed to get more involved. I had also impressed upon the people in charge, that my first dig, had been for the Archaeological Society of Kent. I was now back in Sevenoaks, which was part of the same society.

In the year 1120 A.D., Sevenoaks became a market town. The town grew from a small hamlet, to a bustling metropolis. People, not only came to town to do their shopping, they came to town, to stay. It also meant that the church, St. Bartholomew's, expanded, in all directions.

In 1993, St. Bartholomew's was putting a tea room in their basement. This required all the bodies, buried in the church basement, to be dug up and reburied in the graveyard, adjacent to the church. For archaeological purposes, they were looking for the original walls of the church.

The first assignment they found for me was down on my hands and knees with a trowel. It was now my turn to scrape away, layer by layer, in the hopes of finding bodies. All bones found, or parts thereof, were saved. In one instance, I started to uncover a skull, only to find out, it was half a skull. For me, there was a surge of excitement. It was not like grave digging (as my friend, Amanda, had accused me of doing) as much as digging up a slice of history. It was backbreaking, yet energizing work, and by the end of the day, I felt I had the physical appearance of the Hunchback of Notre Dame.

There were many jobs to be filled and since they felt I was a jack of all trades, I got a variety of assignments. When enough bones had been unearthed, a medical doctor was brought in, for the day, and we worked together. He was identifying the bones and we were repacking all leg bones together, all arm bones together, fingers were differentiated from toes, skulls, or pieces of skulls were bagged separately and all waited for a new final resting place, outside, in the church yard.

I also spent several days wrapping the metal fittings from coffins, in special paper, to keep them from corroding.

The time was up. I had to return to Canada long before this assignment was completed. The three months had passed quickly.

I realized that my life, whether I enjoyed it or not, would also pass quickly. The trip was an unqualified success and I had established a life for myself, as a solo traveler.

One day, I felt sure, I would enjoy it.

Skeena as an adult in Paws For The Comedienne

Bridel Veil Falls, Valdez Road, Alaska

Portage Glacier and Icebergs, Seward Highway, Alaska

Dreaded Taylor Highway. Picture taken while driving.

End of the Alaska Highway, Delta Junction, Alaska

Poor fellow has no idea how lost he really is.
Picture taken in Skagway, Alaska.

Proof that Santa Claus really exists. Picture taken in North Pole, Alaska.

Archaeological Site, Myra, Turkey

View in the heart of Kas, Turkey

An outside view - Old -New Synagogue - Prague

Inside the Old-New Synagogue - Prague

Old cemetery in Prague

Author Joei C. Hossack at Exit Glacier, Seward, Alaska.

Lead Me Not.....

I was not surprised to see a woman, with an old golden retriever, seeing eye dog, asking a couple for directions to one of the smaller restaurants, since the Scarborough Town Center was such a large shopping plaza in North Toronto. When the couple didn't know where the restaurant was, the blind woman left.

Forty minutes later, after a totally unsuccessful shopping expedition, I passed the restaurant and the woman, with the dog, was fifty yards ahead of me. I knew she had walked right by the front door.

I rushed to catch up to her. "Excuse me, are you still looking for the restaurant?" I asked. When she said "yes", I put my arm out and suggested to her, that she take it. "You walked right by the front door" I said. "You are just going to have to teach your dog to read," I commented jokingly. "He knows exactly where it is, I meet my friends there every couple of days" she said, very matter of factly. "He's just pissed off because I won't take him for a ride on the escalator."

The Date from Hell

There is always a point at which, on a date, you will NOT get out of the car and walk home. They had just hit that spot when the topic of conversation changed abruptly. "Everything you really need to know," he said, "is in the Bible". "In the Bible, what the hell are you talking about?" Susan asked. "How did we get from archaeological digging in Egypt, to the Bible," Susan questioned, her voice taking on an unfamiliar and harsh tone. Oh my God, she thought, here he was.....THE DATE FROM HELL.

Susan and Carl had met a couple of years before, at the Community Park Association dance. The only reason he had caught her eye, was because, he always seemed to be dancing. Although Susan had not dated since she was widowed, she loved dancing and her Saturday nights were spent at the Community Park. Besides, she thought, he definitely was amongst the younger men, at the dance. They had danced from time to time, nothing more.

One particular evening, they sat and talked together. Traveling seemed to be the one thing they had in common, so they talked traveling. Since Susan had spent the previous summer on three archaeological digs, they talked archaeology awhile. He seemed very knowledgeable and, for the first time, in a long time, she felt content just to sit and talk. By the end of the evening, they had talked the night away. She had mentioned that she was a seasonal resident and would be leaving soon, but when he invited her to dinner, she accepted.

Carl called on Monday, for dinner on Wednesday. Since they both knew she would be leaving Florida on Friday, she accepted. She did not feel ready for any involvements, but her refrigerator was practically empty, and she felt the timing for a simple dinner, was perfect.

He arrived on time - always a good start. He held the car door open for her - another plus. He started talking. He talked about the weather, at first, and then mentioned the fact that he had had a little trouble finding her place. He told Susan that he was a very avid reader. With each word, the car is moving toward the dinner location. He reads four newspapers every morning, he said and that's where he learned about the archaeology that is currently going on in Egypt. At this point in the conversation, they were approximately two miles away from her home. "BUT," he said, "everything you really need to know, is in the Bible."

"The Bible," her voice taking on the sound of a word totally foreign to her. "How the hell did we get from Egypt to the Bible?" she asked. Wrong question to ask. When Carl started to explain, Susan politely changed the subject. With every third sentence, he spoke about the Bible. Susan became upset - didn't bother Carl. Susan became angry - didn't bother Carl. Didn't work, either.

The evening was a disaster. Carl talked. Susan didn't. It ended early and once back at her home - Susan was rude. Pure and simple. She thanked him for dinner and slammed the door of her condominium.

END OF STORY.

Not on your life.

That Friday, Susan left Florida. It was the 15th of April. She returned to Florida on November 1st, and, as always, to a mountain of mail. During her absence, a package from Carl, had arrived. She didn't have to open it, to know what it contained, but she opened it anyway. All for me, she thought sarcastically, my very own Bible.

While still in a very annoyed state of mind

she wrote Carl the following note: " When I return to Florida after six months of being away, I have enough junk mail to fill a garbage bag. Your book is now part of that garbage bag." Susan then took the book and delivered it to the free, already well stocked library, located in the clubhouse of her condominium. She knew that someone would cherish the book.

At the dance, the following Saturday night, she met up with Carl, who was most annoyed with her for destroying the book.

She never did confess. She enjoyed the humor of it all. He will have to spend the money, to buy the book that this story is published in, to find out what really happened.

Vive La Difference

"You're going to have to leave your little girlfriend now and come inside," she said to her husband, just loud enough for me to overhear. "Little girlfriend." "Little girlfriend!" Those words echoed in my brain until I wanted to scream. That "little girlfriend" the woman was talking about was me; and I was certainly nobody's "little girlfriend".

This was my first night in a campground, by myself, on a journey that would last about six months. "What a terrible way to start," I thought. As the anger subsided, I suddenly felt sick at heart.

I had left a friend's house in Beeton, Ontario, Canada, that morning and by late afternoon had crossed the border into Michigan. I had stopped early. I needed time to figure out how everything worked in my motorhome. The van was relatively new to me, and I not only had to prepare dinner, I had to figure out how to put up the top on the van. I also had to unpack some groceries and to figure out where everything could be stored. "Beside," I thought, "I'm in no hurry." It was still May and not all the campgrounds were in business. The first open campground I came to, after crossing the border into the United States, was a State Park.

After paying the park and camping fees at the main gate, I pulled into one of the many available spots. The one I chose was close to the restrooms and to other campers. I leveled the van as best I could, turned the motor off and breathed a huge sigh of relief. I was home for the night. I sat immobilized, holding onto the steering wheel, and staring straight ahead, for a moment. I could feel the first signs of depression. I had to move before the depression took hold or got worse.

I got out of the van, locked the doors and surveyed the scene. The place was clean and there were just a few campers around. There was a large group of people opposite me, and they had taken my picnic table. They waved to greet me and when they offered to return the picnic table immediately, I said there was no rush. After plugging in my electricity and popping the top on my VW, Westfalia, I went for a walk.

I walked the campground and the wooded paths until I felt at peace. I also felt the beginnings of a hunger pang. I had made it through my first day of driving, without too many tears. Alaska, which was my ultimate goal, was a trip that my husband and I had wanted to take together. He had been an avid fisherman and loved the outdoors, but he was gone, and this was just one of the many trips that I felt I had to take, even if I was alone.

The walk cleared my mind, slightly and I sauntered back to my camping spot, to busy myself and to cook dinner. With the help of a brand new pressure cooker, the chicken in sauce over rice with mushrooms, did not take long to prepare, but eating alone was difficult. If I was to enjoy the next few months, I thought, I had better get used to doing many things alone. I ate in silence, a book propped open on my lap. I sat on a deck chair, just outside my sliding side door.

As I was putting the last of the dinner dishes away, the oldest man in the group at the camping spot across from me, called and motioned for me to come over. "Are you alone?" he asked, sure that I was. "Bring your chair over to the fire, and sit with us a bit." I did not need much in the way of encouragement. I thanked him, folded up my chair and carried it over to the fire. I smiled, nodded and introduced myself. A few introduced themselves and I unfolded my chair in a spot close to the fire. It felt wonderful, since a little dampness, had crept into the air.

The older members of the group, I learned,

were the only ones occupying the camping spot. All the others were visitors: three daughters, two husbands, children and a few friends from a town nearby. They seemed to get along well and none seemed to mind that I had joined them. But they did not say much to me. I just listened.

Gradually, it got darker and colder. Most of the guests said goodbye and went home. The wife of the old man, left and joined another family of campers at their campsite. I sat, listening to the husband and his friend. The conversation was not terribly interesting, but since I was being ignored anyway, I felt I would stay and enjoy the fire. "Besides," I thought, "if I left, I would be sitting alone in my van," and I was not quite prepared for that. The evening was still early and the fire was warm, so I stayed, saying almost nothing.

When his friend left, Jim started talking to me. The reason for the family gathering, he explained, was due to his illness. His body was swollen with cancer and from chemotherapy, he said. He anguished over the swelling in his legs, on the fact that he could hardly walk and over the loss of his hair. He talked quietly while I listened.

When he asked why I was traveling alone, I told him. It was at that time that his wife returned and made the remark, "you're going to have to leave your little girlfriend now and come inside." "I'll be in shortly," he said. She repeated the statement, adamantly. My heart sank.

Jim and I never returned to our topic of conversation and I could not wait to get back to my van. I was close to tears. These were the first people I had spoken to all day and needed just to talk or be with people a while. I said good night softly and walked toward my van. My eyes filled with tears before I unlocked the door of my van.

I made my bed, turned on my black-and-white television set and allowed the tears to come, hoping to fall asleep. My mind worked overtime. I had lost a beautiful, fifty-two year old, husband to a heart attack, so naturally I wanted to run off with a seventy year old, three hundred pound man, suffering from cancer. " How could I resist?" I spat the words out sarcastically, under my breath. "Little girlfriend, indeed," suddenly feeling angry.

Everyone at the next camping spot was outside the following morning. While they busied themselves with breakfast, I packed up and left without saying a word to anyone. No one made an attempt to say good bye to me.

I spent a good part of the day thinking about the events of the previous day. I cried a bit, because I was sure that this sort of reaction would occur my entire trip. When I wasn't weeping, I was laughing, that at fifty years old, gray haired and thirty pounds overweight, the old hag considered me a vamp, that would run off with her man.

The more I thought about the unpleasant incident, the more I was reminded of the trip, I had taken the previous year. I spent three months traveling through Turkey alone and one particular day sprang to mind.

I had discovered the wonderful little resort town of Kas, in the south of Turkey. The area is called the Turquoise Coast, because of the magnificent color of the water. The scenery was breathtaking, the food was as tasty as I had ever experienced, and the people were charming. The town was filled with tourists, and everyone, tourist and local, spoke some degree of English. Kas became the base for my entire Turkish adventure. Since everyone was friendly, I had no problem meeting people.

This particular day, as on most days, I had my morning meal at a little outdoor cafe called Cafe Corner. Abdullah " Apo" -- a handsome, twenty year old, charmer, was my waiter. He took all orders with a certain flourish that guaranteed him a good tip, but the younger and prettier you were, the more attention he lavished on you. When the young and pretty weren't around, he flirted with whomever was there.

I gave him the order for my yogurt breakfast. It consisted of a layer of fresh fruit, a layer of yogurt, over the fruit and topped with honey and nuts. My morning drink was a large cup of appletea. When the breakfast arrived, a couple seated at the next table eyed it and the conversation started immediately. "Yes, it's wonderful," I said, "and very fresh and I never know what fruit will be on the bottom." They both ordered the yogurt.

From their accent, I knew they were from England and they introduced themselves as Margaret and Lyle. They could not decipher my accent and after telling them my name, I explained that I live part of the year in the United States and part of the year in Canada.

By the time we discussed where we were from, what we had seen in Turkey, how long we were visiting, where we were staying, with jokes added to the conversation, the hours passed. Perhaps it was the hectic afternoon of drinking tea, talking and laughing, or the fact that the temperature was 120 degrees, we felt we needed a rest and by mid afternoon were ready to head back to our rooms. Before retiring for a nap, they suggested we meet later that day for dinner. I accepted.

Since the rooms were just as hot as the outdoors, by early evening, we were back at Cafe Corner. We had a drink of sour cherry juice (visne) and soda over ice, another refreshing treat I could introduce them to, and then went to their favorite restaurant for dinner. The evening consisted of lighthearted conversation interspersed with jokes, with my telling most of the jokes. Once I got started and had an audience, that enjoyed my humor, I dredged up jokes. Some of the jokes went back to my childhood, but that made it all the funnier.

During dinner, my companions mentioned that some friends of theirs were arriving the next day from England and they wanted me to meet them. "Let's meet at Cafe Corner in the afternoon, and then we'll decide where we'll go for dinner." I was surprised by the invitation and told them so. "This would rarely happen in America," I said. "Single woman are shunned by couples," I told them.

"Listen," said Marg, "I have been married to this old fart for thirty-five years." "I know everything that is going to come out of his mouth." "You, on the other hand, are refreshing and funny and I know our friends would love to meet you."

"Thank you, yes, I would love to meet your friends, and join you for dinner," I answered. That evening ended late. After dinner, at one restaurant, we had a few drinks at Cafe Corner and then coffee at another spot.

That evening and the following evening were some of the many highlights of my trip to Turkey. There were five of us for dinner that night and their friends, Richard and Cleo, matched my jokes with jokes that I had never heard before. I could not remember when I had laughed so hard and for so long.

What a change, I thought, from my night in the State Park. I had always assumed that campers were so friendly. It hurt to be wrong.

Vive La Difference.

A Simple Act of Kindness

This simple act of kindness took place on my solitary driving trip to Alaska, in the summer of 1995.

I enjoyed my time traveling alone, but it did get lonely sometimes and it was not always easy keeping myself buoyed up and in the right frame of mind to meet people. The time of year was not an easy one for me either. The day before had been the third anniversary of my husband's death. I was now wandering through Yellowstone National Park, before returning to my camping spot in Colter Bay, Grand Teton National Park.

I still had about twenty-five miles to drive when the rain started, slowly at first. Just spitting, in fact. The intermittent windshield wipers took care of the problem, but only momentarily. I found myself under a horrendous black cloud and no matter how fast my windshield wipers worked, they couldn't keep up with the deluge. The change was sudden and frightening. I could barely see and my right wiper started causing problems. The wiper still worked but not in tandem with the other one. One touch from the out of kilter wiper and the good wiper started causing problems. My God, what was happening! This was not the time nor the place.

The rain increased and the roads became treacherous, with water and mud forming pools in spots, all over the road. I pulled off to the side. My heart was pounding so hard that my ears hurt. I had to get back to my campsite. It was dark and getting on toward night. I had to keep moving. I shifted to second gear and inched my way, putting my wipers on only when I really couldn't see and, even then, just once. The passenger side wiper finally died. Each time I turned the wiper on, I prayed, "please let me get through this nightmare."

As if by magic, the minute I left Yellowstone National Park and entered the Grand Teton, the sun came out. Glorious, bright, warm. I was safe. Still shaken by the fierceness and velocity of the storm, I kept moving, slowly. I found my campground and camping site and as soon as I turned off the motor, my heart stopped pounding.

I relaxed awhile with a cup of tea and started preparing dinner. My stomach was uneasy, but once relaxed, I would still need to eat something for dinner. While my homemade soup simmered on the stove, I checked my VW manual There was a Volkswagen dealership in Jackson, Wyoming, forty miles south of the Grand Teton National Park. I breathed a sigh of relief. Not only would I get my windshield wiper repaired, but Jackson and Jackson Hole were on my list of places to visit. I would kill two birds with one stone.

After an early breakfast the next morning, I headed for the dealership in Jackson. The VW dealer had become a GEO dealer. I asked if there was a VW dealer in town. "No," said the young executive behind the glass window, "what's the problem?" I explained what had happened. "I had a VW once, let me check," he said. With a wrench, he tightened the bolt. He guaranteed that it would solve the problem. "The wipers on the VW are designed to loosen before they damage the motor," he explained. The passenger side did indeed work. When I offered to pay, he held up his hand. "No problem," he said. In my moment of grateful relief, I forgot to mention that the wiper on the driver's side also needed tightening. Shortly after leaving the GEO dealer, I tested the wipers. The driver's side wiper was loose. "Never mind," I thought, grateful to be on my way, " I would have it fixed at my next gas fill up."

I took the long way back to Colter Bay, stopping long enough to enjoy the scenery and a bit of lunch. The spectacular landscape, the result of eons of glaciers and earthquakes, had produced the Teton Range; however, now black clouds started to engulf the mountains. While I stood in cool sunshine, I watched through binoculars as a raging blizzard covered the highest peaks on the mountain. When the first droplets pelted my face, I returned to the van and drove on.

Safely back at the campground, I watched a mother, father and three sons move into the site behind mine. They unloaded a motorbike and within minutes, mother and youngest son belched away, leaving behind a stream of smoke and the rest of the family, to start setting up camp. When mother and son returned, the other two lads took a spin on the bike. When the boys returned, father and another son whizzed by and disappeared around the corner. This went on for over an hour, and when I saw an opportunity, I approached the father. “You know,” I said, after introducing myself, “I have never known anyone, who owned a motorbike, that did not have a complete set of ratchet tools.” “Jim Bolton,” he said, “what do you need?’

While he tightened my windshield wiper, we talked about the camping spots, then he asked if I was traveling alone. Although, I didn’t want my traveling alone to be common knowledge, I nonetheless, said “yes”. “Please join us for dinner,” he said. I thanked him for his kind invitation. At six o’clock, when I saw his wife outside cooking, I approached. “Are you aware that your husband is inviting strange women for dinner?”

“Yes,” she said, introducing herself as Joan, “and we are expecting you.” Before resuming KP duties, she introduced me to sons, Scott, John and Tim.

I joined them at their picnic table, and brought along a huge pot of piping hot, homemade soup and the remains of a bottle of wine. We gathered around the table and started dinner with the soup and fresh bread. We had spaghetti, salad and dessert. When my wine was finished, Jim opened a bottle of theirs. We told stories and shared experiences in the wild. Just before dark, we told ghost stories. As night fell, we moved closer to the bonfire. When we had consumed more food and drink then was reasonable or necessary, at any given meal, I was introduced to S'mores -- a toasted marshmallow, with a piece of chocolate, sandwiched between two graham crackers. Sweet enough to keep any dentist in business the entire length of his career, but delicious.

This simple evening, with a wonderful family, is one of my treasured memories on a trip that started with a frightened, but determined, middle-aged woman and ended twenty-five thousand miles, and six months later, with the world by the tail.....and a tale to tell the world.

The Last Frontier

I did it! I wanted to shout it from the roof tops. I did it!

When I started on my incredible journey, I had just purchased a slightly used, navy blue, VW, Westfalia, van and was sure I wanted to keep it, in pristine condition. I would wash it. I would clean out the interior. I would keep it free from debris and I certainly would not plaster it with slogans and bumper stickers; however, after completing seven weeks of traveling, not only the Alaska Highway, but the Richardson Highway to Chitina, the George Parks Highway from Anchorage to Fairbanks, the Glenn Highway from Tok to Anchorage, the Haines Highway from Haines to Haines Junction, Yukon Territory, the Klondike Highway from Skagway, Alaska back to the Alaska Highway, the Seward, the Sterling, the Tagish, the dreaded Taylor, with its twenty-three miles of mud instead of a road, and last but not least, the Top of the World Highway, I now feel that I would love to plaster, every visible inch of the vehicle, with signs that say "I did it".

For those who have braved traveling, in the land of the Last Frontier, as their license plates indicate, you know the thrill of it. For those who have not, I must dig down to the bottom of my toes for the courage, to describe it. I don't ever remember feeling smaller than in Alaska, where everything was so vast and intimidating.

The Alaska Highway starts in Dawson Creek, British Columbia and, for me, getting there was a feat in itself, since I started on my adventurous route in Sarasota, Florida. A giant marker, in the center of Dawson Creek indicates the start of the Alaska Highway. This is milepost "0" and despite what the post says, the end of the Alaska Highway is Delta Junction at mile 1,422. Don't tell that to the people of Fairbanks who think the road ends in their fair city.

Dawson Creek is a small, pleasant community. It is an easy walking town, with a wonderful museum and pioneer village. Shown daily, or possibly hourly, at the museum, is a feature film depicting the construction of the Alaska Highway in its entirety, or so they would like you to believe. I know better now, but I watched the film with intense interesting, hoping to see the highway, fully completed. The U.S. government started the highway in 1942 and used it as a means of getting supplies to the soldiers stationed at bases in Alaska. I'm sure the road may be completed sometime during my lifetime; but, it still has a long way to go.

In Dawson Creek, my van was outfitted with a metal and mesh screen to guard against rocks and bugs and to protect the headlights, so when I got on the road heading north, I was feeling rather confident.

The people I had met in the campground in Dawson Creek were all motorhomers and when referring to the Alaska Highway, they spoke either in awe of it, and with a tremendous amount of trepidation, because they had not started their journey yet. We were all either talking excitedly, yet apprehensively, about going "up" the highway or they were telling horrors stories, about dozens of flat tires, broken windshields, broken axles or getting bogged down in mud deep enough to cover your wheels, while touring Alaska before coming "down" the highway. Either way, we shared our experiences.

Since many had expressed their concern about my traveling alone and invited me to tag along behind, it was a relief, to see so many campers. I knew that if anything should go amiss, campers were wonderful, caring people and would not leave a woman, traveling alone, stranded by the side of the road.

I left Dawson Creek the following morning and passed Fort St. John, on my way north. I camped, that night, in Fort Nelson. Again, I was relieved to see so many people, and most of them were going north. There were many people to share, not only my experiences with, but when another van, exactly like mine, pulled in beside me, we shared a wonderful evening.

Pete, Joanne and I shared some travel experiences, some similar problems with the van we both owned, a couple of bottles of wine, dinner, and the following morning we each had our share of one gigantic, headache. Fortunately we did not have far to drive the next day. We ended up, in different campgrounds, but both campgrounds were in Liard Hot Springs.

Since hot tubs are a special passion of mine, I could not resist soaking for hours, letting the mineral water wash over me and cleanse my body, my mind and renew my wine-soaked, spirit.

Feeling much better after dinner, I spent several hours, that evening, wandering the same marshy area in the hopes of seeing an elusive moose, that frequented the area. Since most of the people were in small groups or in pairs, I wandered the area alone and only after I returned to my camper, did I realize that it was after eleven o'clock in the evening. I went to sleep that night, for the first time, while it was still light outside.

Since the campground was a short walk from the hot springs, I returned the next morning for another dose of relaxation and by the time I got onto the highway, I was prepared to anything, almost.

It did not take long that morning to run into my first bit of construction and gravel. The truck drivers did not live by the same rules, that other drivers do. While the passenger cars, campers, motorhomes and vans did their best to go slowly, stay as far to the right as possible and even show courtesy, a few approaching truckers did not and within an hour, on this gravel road, I knew my windshield would need replacing. Three different trucks heading toward me, had been traveling so fast that the rocks, spinning out from under their wheels, smashed into my windshield. They hit with the force of a bullet and shattered not only my windshield, but my nerves and my confidence, as well. I cringed each time a vehicle came too close or seemed to be traveling too fast, coming toward me.

I was relieved when I reached Whitehorse in the Yukon Territory. I began to look upon this as a magical, but very intimidating, land. I had entered a world that most people only read about. Some mortgage their home for a week or two on a cruise ship to see the Inside Passage of Alaska. If they are lucky, they fly to Anchorage and then drive to Denali National Park and possibly Fairbanks. Others, let someone else do the driving and choose one of the many bus tours to Homer or Seward or Valdez. But not me. I had driven, by myself, from the west coast of Florida to Whitehorse, camping all the way.

In the seven weeks that I traveled the area, I discovered, not only a land where the sun never sets, but mountain peaks so high, they look down at the clouds, majestically and are never without a crown of snow. I have walked on glaciers, touched icebergs, saw waterfalls cascading down from the heavens and watched ice worms wriggling about, knowing that a touch of my finger, would incinerate them. I have talked with people who have a pioneer spirit that rival those of the Klondike Gold Rush. I have been where moose, caribou, bear and lynx still cause traffic jams and where dogs are not only man's best friend, but the only link to the outside world, in winter.

I have a certificate, with my name on it and the date, I completed driving the Alaska Highway, that I will display in a prominent place so anyone seeing it, will know that I am not an ordinary mortal and that I have driven the highways of hell and survived. I now feel, for brief moments, that I may have acquired a bit of that pioneer spirit, that is so prevalent in the Last Frontier.

My time here is at a close. It is the end of August and I am told winter can come at any time and I do not want to be trapped in the north country. I have witnessed vastness beyond my wildest imagination. I have an incredible story to tell, but my journey is only half complete. I must leave and head for home.

The Hands That Heal

To feel the warmth of someone's hands. A stranger's hands, yet gentle and familiar, with only a touch of longing as they caress and soothe, and the last bit of tension, evaporates. "It's over," Andrew whispered, "relax".

"What a fabulous ploy," Jeanne thought, when she arrived.

"Come on in," Andrew shouted from the second story window, "I'll be down in a minute."

Finding a three dimensional puzzle on the table, in the waiting room, her fingers played with the pieces, until she found one that fit.

"Hi," said Andrew, "ready for your massage?"

"Sure" Jeanne replied, with a smile, while her insides turned to jelly. "I've never done this before," she thought, "what the heck am I doing here?"

It had all started the day before. She knew she had seen Andrew at the museum, on several occasions, over the last couple of years, where they both volunteered. He always appeared shy, not talking much, and until yesterday, had never spoken to her. When she did hear him speak, it was always softly.

She knew, also, from the chit chat at the coffee breaks, that he had lost his spouse about the same time that she had been widowed. They shared a common sorrow, but while Andrew was soft spoken and gentlemanly, she was loud and saucy, always talking traveling.

She had noticed him the week before, when he sat behind her, at the Monday morning briefing. The first time he had actually spoken to her was yesterday. YESTERDAY, for God's sake. He asked where her next trip would be? Jeanne told him, that she had promised her sister, she would stay in North America, so they could visit for a while; however, she remarked, " I would love to go somewhere exotic, like Viet Nam or Egypt." She told Andrew about her new writing career and that she wanted something exciting, and foreign, to write about.

He told her about becoming a licensed massage therapist and "would you like a massage?" he asked, handing her a business card. "Call me," he said.

Up close and smiling, "he's really cute," was all Jeanne could think about, as she pointed and tapped on her shoulders. Andrew rubbed her shoulders gently, but firmly. "I'll give you a week or two to stop that," she quipped and didn't move for a moment, in the hopes he would continue.

First things first, she thought - work, and took a step forward. "Thanks," said Jeanne with an air of nonchalance, "that felt great" and left to start what would be a long, busy, day.

She slept well that night. But she could not stop thinking about how sensuous it felt to have Andrew's hands on her shoulders. She telephoned him, before her courage could fail her.

In three hours, she would be lying naked on a massage table. With effort, she pushed those thoughts to the back of her mind. She knew she wanted to enjoy life and to experience everything. She wanted to treat herself to all the fine things that this world had to offer, before it was too late. She knew, also, it had been too long since she had experienced the healing powers of touch.

* * * * *

The room she entered was small, but warm and cozy. From the desk, she picked up, and examined, the bottle of lotion, while the music played softly, in the background.

"Take off whatever clothes you would feel comfortable taking off." "Most people remove everything," Andrew volunteered from the next room.

For a moment, Jeanne felt the urge to cover up, to hide herself from the fifty year old body, that belonged to her. "He is really cute," she thought embarrassingly, "do I really want him to see me like this?" but she stripped, putting her clothes neatly on the awaiting chair, and crawled under the cover, on the massage table.

Understanding her tension, Andrew was at her side, giving instructions, as soon as Jeanne said "ready" in a voice that was quietly hesitant.

Through nervousness, she talked weather, and travel, and the museum, and anything else that came to mind; but, the first question was, if he had just taken his hands out of the freezer? They both laughed, just enough to ease a little of the tension.

His hands were warm, and starting at her head, he massaged her scalp before gently sliding down to her face. His fingers soothed her forehead and she could feel the tension slowly ebbing.

Before realizing it, tears filled her eyes and cascaded down the side of her face, as Andrew's hands continued to caressed her temple, her cheeks and finally her chin and neck. "It's OK," Andrew whispered softly, "it's just a release of tension, it's OK".

Jeanne could feel life returning to every pore, as his fingers gently massaged the back of her neck, before sliding down under her back, lifting her upper body, ever so slightly.

"I'll do all the work," said Andrew softly, "you don't have to move," as he slipped to her right side and uncovered her arm. The lotion was warm and it was spread liberally. The length of her arm was stroked. The kneading, started at the shoulder, and slowly worked its way down to her hand, and then to each finger and for a moment, time stood still. Gently Andrew placed her arm under the security of the cover and maneuvered, effortlessly, to Jeanne's left side, to repeat the process.

Uncovering one leg at a time, the healing touch started at the top of her thigh and ended with her feet being rubbed and individual toes massaged, until all stress, was gone. For brief moments all the tension would ease up, and each time, it would being the uncomfortableness of tears, but she knew she had found a bit of heaven.

His hands were warm and moist with lotion and gliding over her body, kneading and manipulating, warming and caressing.

Occasionally, for a brief moment, she would stop talking long enough to feel the warmth and the sheer joy of being in a world of her own; however, she would soon realize that she was mostly naked, self-consciousness would set in, and she would be off babbling again.

Gently, but firmly, Andrew rested his hands, on her back, not moving. The massage was over. A glow descended over her body as she lay still, warmed by the experience of true pleasure. "Why have I never done this before?" she wondered.

Intimidation

"What are you going to talk about?" asked the lady seated next to me, with her bandaged leg, propped on an ottoman.

"I spent three months traveling in Turkey in 1994, and I'm going to give a little presentation," I responded.

"Do you have any slides?" she asked innocently.

"No, this is just a lecture," I explained.

"Oh," she retorted, "three weeks ago we had a lady speak about her trip to Kenya and she had over two hundred slides to show us. There were slides of animals and plants and flowers and all kinds of different things. Since you have no slides, do you have some pictures to show us?" she asked.

"No," I replied, as confidently as I could, looking in all directions for any possible escape route. I was about to present my first lecture and I suddenly had the feeling, that I was standing there naked.

Six weeks earlier, I had attended a single's evening at the Jewish Community Center in Sarasota, Florida. The guests, in the group, were asked to introduce themselves with their name and a bit of history. Not a problem, I felt. I would give them my life in a nutshell. When it was my turn, I stood. I gave them my name. I told the group that I was a seasonal resident in Sarasota, that I spend over six months each year traveling and am currently writing my first book. I smiled, nodded to a few individuals who were watching me intently, and sat down.

Before all the introductions were over, I was approached and asked if I would like to give a lecture. "Speak about any trip you want, your choice," said the president of the single's club. Sounded easy enough, especially since I had four months of Toastmaster's (an international speaking organization) under my belt. "This would be wonderful practice," I thought. I accepted, knowing, even though I had just returned from a driving trip to Alaska, I would be speaking about one of my favorite parts of the world, Turkey.

On the day of the lecture, I did everything to buoy up my confidence. I knew there would be questions and I hoped I would be able to answer them. I practiced my speech as best I could, trying to anticipate some of the questions. I dressed smartly and comfortably. I had prepared notes and the start of my book on Turkey, with me. I even had friends, in the audience, who had called to say they were going to be there, just to lend support. I was fully prepared for everything..... everything, that is, except for this little lady, seated on my right, who had just told me, that the last speaker had two hundred slides on Kenya.

The president called the meeting to order. I was introduced as the speaker for the evening and I thanked them all for inviting me.

Since 1994 had been my third attempt at making it to Turkey, I read the start of my book. It explained that in 1991, while on the way to Turkey, my husband Paul and I, got "caught" on the Greek Island of Crete, when the Gulf War erupted. The book touched briefly on the fact that, in 1992, again, on our way to Turkey, we traveled as far as Germany where my husband died of a heart attack. "To fulfill our dream, I went to Turkey alone," I read from the typed pages. "Although I was terrified," the book explained, "I got off the plane at 4:10 in the morning at the Dalaman Airport and started an adventure, that ended three months later with loving the country and the people." Slides or no slides, I had them. They were listening.

The talk became a little less formal. Once into the swing of speaking in front of the group, and knowing I had their full attention, it was thrilling. I relaxed enough to really enjoy the lecture. I even managed to stop and answer questions, from time to time, and had no problem getting back to the organized part of the lecture, that had been prepared.

A few members in the group of thirty or so, knew I had just returned from Alaska and while I talked about Ankara, they wanted to talk about Anchorage. As gently as I could, and without the aid of a two-by-four, I eased them back onto the subject. One hour and fifteen minutes later, I was losing my audience and ended quickly by saying, "I would love to go back to Turkey, some day. Does anyone want to go with me?" Applause, applause, applause.

After the lecture, some friends approached. They complimented me on how confident I appeared and remarked on how much they enjoyed listening to my animated talk on Turkey. It was only then, that I confessed how intimated I had been, by the lady I heard about, with the 200 slides.

"Did you also hear that we asked her to stop showing the slides after the first hundred or so?" my friend, Sonia, inquired.

"No," I replied.

"Did you also hear that when the lights went on, after the slide presentation, that most of the people in the audience, were asleep?"

"No," I replied chuckling, "my little voice of doom didn't happen to mention that".

Christmas Confusion

Traveling is supposed to be a learning experience. It is supposed to broaden your horizons, to open your mind to all possibilities and to all peoples. It should make a person feel secure in strange countries because all people are basically alike and kind hearted. It is supposed to bring understanding and a certain amount of peace and contentment. Then, why, after seven years of being of the road, for more months than I stay at home, each year, do I feel so totally confused when it comes to Christmas?

After traveling in my motorhome, for many, many months last summer, I graced North Pole, Alaska with my presence, if you'll pardon the pun. I have been told, all my life, that when Santa Claus is not delivering gifts, to all the good little boys and girls, on the night before Christmas, the tiny village of North Pole is where Santa and Mrs. Claus, hang their hats, so to speak. There, Santa spends his day reading his list, and checking it twice, while the elves are busy, in the factory, making all the toys. It is Mrs. Claus' task to care for the reindeer.

Excitement was high, when I arrived at Santa's village. Since there were not many people in line, after all, it was only August, I decided that it was important for me to get a candy cane from Santa himself. I waited my turn. He greeted me warmly, as Santa would, and asked my name. I told him, and added that I had been good all year long, perhaps more by circumstance than by choice, but I was good and "I would like a candy cane," I said.

He patted his lap. "Oh, no" I said, with a chuckle, "I'm much too big for that". He insisted that he could not give me my candy cane unless I sat on his lap. "OK, but don't blame me," I warned, "if you end up with a hernia". How could I refuse Santa

Claus? Besides, there it was, within my grasp, a beautiful, red-and-white stripped, candy cane.

I treasured my prize. I had a candy cane given to me by Santa himself and nothing could have been more delicious. So where's the confusion, you ask?

This year's travels took me to a different part of the world. There I was, revisiting a part of the world that I loved -- Kas, Turkey. I had been there about two weeks, when a friend asked. "Have you seen where Santa Claus comes from?" "Certainly," I said, "I met Santa last year, in North Pole, Alaska". "No, no, no," Michael retorted, "the real Santa Claus". I was stunned. "What do you mean, the REAL Santa Claus?"

"The real Santa Claus", Michael informed me, "was born in Patara, Turkey". I shook my head at him. Poor, demented soul, I thought. Patara, Turkey, indeed. "I've been to Patara," I said, "I saw no evidence of Santa Claus -- all I saw were very impressive archaeological ruins and a wonderful beach".

"Santa Claus was born there," he said. "His fame, however, did not spread until he became the Bishop of Demre," Michael went on to explain.

This, I had to see for myself and couple of days later, we hopped on a bus heading for Demre (Myra). In one hour and fifteen minutes, we were there. At the bus stop, there were signs pointing to the Church of St. Nicholas ("Noel Baba" in Turkish). We walked to the church. Although the church had been restored and offered a rare chance to see what a Fifth Century Byzantine church looked like, this still did not prove that Santa Claus existed.

We visited the church gardens. Lo and behold, there it was -- a huge statue, blackened with age but surrounded by children, standing in the center of the garden -- Santa Claus. "This," said my friend, "is where the legend of Father Christmas began, in the Fourth Century".

Father Nicholas was a Christian bishop who gave anonymous gifts to village girls, who had no dowry. He dropped bags of coins, down the chimney of their houses and the "gift from heaven" would allow them to find husbands and to marry. "This is perhaps why he is the patron saint of virgins," Michael continued. Noel Baba went on to add sailors, children, pawnbrokers and Holy Russia to his flock.

As his fame grew, so did his parish, and the people from the Roman city of Myra, (named for the aromatic plant gum, myrrh) was added to his congregation. Since Myra was a thirty minute walk from Demre, we went to have a look and stayed the rest of the day. We climbed to the rock-hewn tombs and walked the Roman theater, looking over the countryside from several angles. It turned into a wonderful day of exploration, but if he is the REAL Santa Claus -- then where is my candy cane?

Murder and Just a Touch of Cannibalism

Eyes wide in horror, "you killed my baby," screamed Stephen, "you are a murderer and a cannibal."

"I did not, stop saying that," I argued, trying to keep my voice under control. "I did NOT kill your baby."

"You killed it and you ate it," Stephen insisted, "you are a monster," he said, as he went out the door, stomping up the walk.

Shoulders slumped, I watched as he went up the path and over to visit his neighbor. I knew he would spread vicious rumors about me.

I stood there in the doorway, shaking my head in disbelief. "You killed the baby," I said to no one in particular. "I just disposed of the body."

The mystery had started about four weeks before. Stephen walked around his garden at the SEM Villas, overlooking the Turquoise Coast, at his home in Kas, Turkey. Everything looked in order, as he surveyed the landscape, except for one little plant, just outside his front door. The tiny yellow flower had dropped off, and the smallest green stripped watermelon, lay there on the ground. He bent closer to inspect it. He did not remember planting it, but there it was, large, or should I say, small as life, a watermelon, in all its glory.

For four weeks Stephen watered it faithfully every day. He tried to protect it, from the unrelenting Turkish sun. He pointed to it proudly, to anyone who visited.

For four weeks he watered, watched, protected and showed off his baby. For weeks he talked of its future, hoping to display it beside its giant relatives.

Since I hadn't seen the watermelon for a week or so, I was anxious to check on its progress. It was about the size of a baseball.

"Stephen," I yelled from the doorway, "your watermelon is split." "It's useless."

With tears in his eyes, he came to inspect his baby. He lifted it up gently, pulling it from the vine, and brought it into the house.

"Oh dear," he moaned, "the baby is gone, what shall we do with it?"

I relieved him of the object that had caused the extreme sadness, pried it open with my fingers and with the aid of a teaspoon, lifted out the contents.

"Want a bite?" I offered.

"You monster," Stephen yelled, "you killed my baby."

"No," I repeated, "I did not kill your baby. I just disposed of the body." "A bit small," I said, "but really delicious."

Mobile House of Horrors

I am fortunate, by nature, to be one of those very healthy individuals. I make an effort to eat properly. I try to exercise. If I have skipped a few hours sleep at night, I have no qualms about treating myself to an afternoon nap. As a matter of fact, I enjoy an afternoon nap, even if I have not skipped a few hours sleep. I try to balance my life, between work and play, whenever possible.

I find, however, that when I am in pain, it is usually, for some strange reason, self-inflicted. I am referring, of course, to that extra glass of red wine, that produced a migraine headache so horrific, I spent the night on my hands and knees and my head in the toilet bowl. I have also been known to force that bit of extra speed, during a walk-a-thon for charity, that took me to sixteenth place from seventeenth place and caused shin splints so terrible, that even the healing hands of Reiki, did little to ease the pain. Three days later I would still be walking, shall we say, delicately. Even now, when I could so easily have gotten on a plane in London, England and landed in Prague, Czech Republic two hours later, I am in the process of torturing my mind and body, on a bus.

My reason for doing this to myself, at the time, seemed so simple. I had four weeks to kill before I caught my flight from London, England to Toronto, Canada. I wanted to visit a few places that I had not seen before and I wanted to be flexible about the return trip. With a bus, the return portion of the ticket, could be left open and the fee for booking it, would be nominal . I felt, also, that my friend and traveling companion, Jean and I, had a better chance of meeting other people to explore with, if we took a bus. Besides, the lady at the bus station, lied.

We booked the trip at the bus depot in a small town, close to Jean's home, Bath, England. We had trouble getting a reservation for any sooner than the following Monday. Since there were not two seats available on any coach, the entire weekend, we felt that this would be an interesting way to travel. So many others had chosen the same route, we were sure our plan was the right one.

The booking agent made the trip sound marvelous. For twenty-four hours, we were told, we would be on a luxury coach. It seems, I heard the word "luxury" and missed the word "coach". Meals would be served on board, along with snacks and sandwiches. Coffee, tea, milk and soft drinks could be purchased at anytime, and English money would be accepted on board. There would be toilet facilities on board, as well. For me, this was essential, because as soon as I can't, I must.

I booked our trip. May I repeat.....she lied.

* * * * *

Before catching our bus at Victoria Station in London, Jean and I had a five hour car ride, that was done, in two stages. Jean's husband, Bill, insisted that he drive us to our bus.

The first leg of the trip, from Bristol to Swindon, took place the evening before. We camped out overnight with their daughter, Debra and her family, enjoying their hospitality. We relaxed and delighted in an evening of wine, lively conversation, a bit of television and, finally, a hot chocolate before bedtime. We awoke very early the following morning. We scurried around trying not to wake the entire household, dressing as quietly as we could and leaving the house, like a thief in the night, into typical, early morning British dampness. We drove into London while it was still dark and were relieved that only the last half hour of driving, was done in the early morning traffic.

At Victoria Station, we had no trouble finding the bus going to Prague. At first sight, and second and third sights, I might add, I could not believe that I had committed myself, and my friend, to this mobile house of horrors, voluntarily. The seats were as hard as pews and barely reclined. In the true German tradition, the seat part of the chair was so short, and it hit your thigh so far up your leg.....zat you vill sit up straight.

My instinct screamed, GET OUT OF HERE, SAVE YOURSELF, but we had just spent five hours, on two different days, getting to the station. I stifled my instincts with a cup of coffee. Jean stifled hers with a cup of tea. We looked at each other, cursed, laughed and climbed on board. We found some unoccupied seats at the back of the bus. We took them.

To add to our misery, there was no food, no coffee, no tea, no soft drinks. In fact, if you didn't bring it on board, you didn't have it. Fortunately, thanks to Jean's camping experience, we had enough food, junk and otherwise, with us, to supply a starving army on maneuvers. We brought the food because we felt it would cut down on our expenses. We never dreamed that the food we had with us, would have to carry, two ravenous tourists, through four countries.

We missed our usual, hourly, coffee and tea breaks. To make matters worse, the restaurants we stopped at, would not change English coin and if we wanted coffee or tea, we would have to change Sterling notes. In each case, we would have to change at least a five pound bank note, into the currency of that country. Much to our annoyance, the bus stopped often, on our journey. We did not want to cash our hard earned money in France, nor in Belgium, nor in Germany. We waited and would cash what we needed in the Czech Republic. It was a long, dry, thirsty trip.

True to her word; however, there was a toilet on board, to be used only in emergencies. Emergency it would have to be. I don't know when it was last cleaned. It certainly was not cleaned anytime in the month, we were on board.

My friend, Jean, it seems, has the ability to sleep anywhere, including on a hanger in the closet, if it becomes necessary, but not me. When I wasn't trying to make myself comfortable, sitting on the seat or the floor, or trying to lie on two seats or three seats or the floor, or generally twisting or contorting my body into a shape, that it had no possible way of contorting into, I was writing a nasty letter to the bus company. I complimented them on their ability to train their personnel to lie with a straight face.

Also, to add to our miseries, we left England in the rain. Since the majority of the passengers were English, the rain felt, it should make the Britishers feel at home, and it followed us through France and Belgium and just about the time we could enjoy a little sightseeing, night fell and the lights went out. Being an relatively experienced traveler, I made every effort to go out with the lights.

We arrived in Prague at 9:00 A.M. the following morning. Michael Jackson's concert had closed the evening before. That was where we discovered, that it was due to the his concert, that every seat, on every bus, had been sold out, for the previous weekend. I wondered if any of the hundred spires that Prague was famous for, would still be standing?

"Oh my God," suddenly horrified at the realization, we still had the return portion to our bus tickets.

Old Jewish Quarter - Prague

It rained again, on this, our last day, in Prague; but somehow it was fitting to be raining and drab on this day. Today, my friend, Jean, and I visited the Old Jewish Quarter.

Our first stop was the Old-New Synagogue. This temple dates from the year 1270 A.D., or possibly 1280 A.D.. It stands on the original site and is Prague's oldest Gothic monument and one of the oldest, and best preserved, synagogues in Europe. The synagogue's massive stone construction helped it survive in the face of fires, pogroms, floods and other natural disasters. It is still used for prayer services by the Jewish community.

It is Yom Kipper (Day of Atonement) and the synagogue will be closing at 2:00 P.M. today, Sunday, September 22. It had been our plan to go through this part of the tour first, because of the early closing; however, when we looked at our ticket, we realized that each of the different museums had a time stamp on it and we must go through this portion first or we will not be admitted.

Once inside, I am resentful of the extra money paid to visit the Old-New Synagogue ($8.00 U.S.) because it is our last day in Prague and we could have budgeted the money elsewhere. The temple is so small and barren that it doesn't seem worth it. Before entering the main part of the temple, we noticed a small enclosed block house at the back and I asked another tourist if she knew what the house was used for. She was reading a guide book, found the proper page, and explained that when additions or funding was needed for the synagogue, the money was placed there for safekeeping. "The Jews were also very heavily taxed," she explained, "and that was where the money was kept."

"Considering what it cost to get in here," I

said, "we're still heavily taxed," and both she and my friend Jean chuckled, a little louder than to themselves.

Inside the house of worship, even with so many people around, Jean and I decided we wanted to "feel" the peace. We sat and tried to meditate but found there were too many people milling around and we could not concentrate. We sat and looked, taking it all in: the speaker's tribune, with the interior divided into two naves (political and religious); the red banner, with the Star of David and the pointed hat, which was given to the community for helping Ferdinand I defend against the Swedes in the year 1648; the slots in the windows for women to view the services, but not to participate. And, as is our favorite, we watched the people.

From the Old-New Synagogue we went to the Maislova Synagogue. Mordecai Maisel bought the land in the year 1590, to build his own house of worship. In its time, the Maislova Synagogue was the most revered shul in the community. Many of the artifacts, housed there, were donated by Mr. & Mrs. Maisel. Like many other synagogues, it was destroyed by fire and rebuilt, more simply, in 1691. Mordecai Maisel did not live to see the new temple. He died in 1601.

From Maislova, we walked around the corner to Pinkas Synagogue, dedicated to the people of Czechoslovakia who died in the holocaust. The synagogue was empty of artifacts and painted pure white, as a symbol of mourning. In single file, behind many others, Jean and I walked through, silently. The words heard in the background, spoken in whispers.

The name of each victim was inscribed on the walls. Seventy-seven thousand, two hundred and ninety-seven names, all printed perfectly. The family name printed only once and the given names and dates followed. Wall after wall after wall. Name after name after name Everything lettered perfectly - their name, the date they were born and the date of their deportation to the death camp. A little plaque, hanging on a rope, standing two feet away from the wall, signifies what city, town or village the victims came from. Their entire existence, printed in one small space, on a wall. The experience was numbing. I had never come so close to the horror.

While Jean shook her head and commented, over and over, whispering the birth dates of the children, my eyes went from name to name, looking for mine. Only one name came close; but, my family background is Rumanian.

The second floor is the same as the first. The third floor is the same as the first and the second, but we are compelled to go. We go, even if it is just to say, "we know you lived". We are paying our respects.

My flippancy of earlier in the day was gone. Jean and I walked in silence. Tears filled our eyes. So many people. So very many people. We talked and shared our feelings, for a few moments in the courtyard, before continuing our tour. I was not prepared for this. How does a person prepare themselves for horror?

From the Pinkas Synagogue, we walked around the corner to the Old Jewish Cemetery. People were buried in this cemetery as early as the thirteenth century, with the last grave dug in the year 1787. There seems to be no order here. This is one of the most unusual, macabre cemeteries anywhere. A surreal configuration of leaning, fallen and crammed-together gravestones combine to total twelve thousand stones above ground, with up to sixty thousand graves, in as many as twelve layers, below ground. Some headstones are in urgent need of repair, while other are standing erect, visible and prominent.

We found the tombs of Maisel, principle figure in building and renovating Jewish buildings and homes during the Renaissance and Rabbi Lowe, the most learned Talmudic scholar in Jewish history. There were many tourists around, and I took the time to explain why little pebbles had been placed on some of the headstones. "Even when I visit my mother and father in a cemetery in Montreal, Canada, I place a little pebble on their gravestone to say, I was there," I explained. It is simply a sign of respect and remembrance.

After leaving the cemetery, we entered the adjacent building. It is the Jewish Museum building and it is the home of pictures. The pictures came from Terezin, about an hour north of Prague. Terezin was Hitler's model city. The Jews were evacuated from Prague and ghettoed there. They lived, worked, studied, painted, wrote, attended school and where they were viewed by the rest of the world. Once seen, they were sent to other concentration camps or executed at Terezin.

All the paintings, drawings, stories, poems and memorabilia were saved. Some paintings, bold and complex, were by Jewish artists. Some, simple and naive, drawn by Jewish children. The Old Jewish Quarter in Prague is the best preserved in the world. Hitler wanted it that way. This was to be "The Museum of an Extinct People".

Somehow it seemed fitting that it was raining in Prague, on this, our last day.

That evening Jean and I attended Yom Kipper Services at the Spanish Temple in Prague. The rain stopped.

The Witness

I was coming to the end of my morning constitutional and approaching an old house, badly in need of painting. A large, leafless, oak tree filled with air plants, sat on one side of the property. It was surrounded by an unkempt lawn. I froze.

Staring in fascinated horror, I found myself rooted to the spot, as a snowy egret grabs a snake in its beak. Over and over it picks up the snake, holding it momentarily. The limbless serpent coils its body around the bird's beak. The snake is released with a little toss of the bird's head. The bird retrieves its prize over and over. And once again, the snake is tossed. The bird moves and darts and attacks, careful to avoid the head of the snake, in its struggle for life.

I stare, as each time the foot long reptile is picked up, it becomes less and less aggressive. The Great Egret holds its ground, keeping the snake in its beak, longer and longer. The snake becomes less prone to movement. Gradually it no longer winds and twists. It just hangs, writhing slowly in the dance of death.

Even before death has descended, the egret starts to swallow, inch by inch. I watch as the entire snake disappears. I watch as the neck of the egret bulges in spots and the bulges move to accommodate the snake, that is still showing signs of life, even as it descends into hell.

My mind is reeling. Am I being prepared for my trip to Southeast Asia, where the food might be different from my usual menu?

Some Day My Prince Will Come

I had had a wonderful night's sleep and for the first time in seven months, that great night's sleep was in my own bed, in my own house, in Sarasota, Florida.

After fidgeting, fussing, and fuming for forty-one hours on a bus, from Toronto, Canada to Sarasota, I had actually slept in, and crawled out of, my bed at 8:00 A.M.. Never had I slept so long.

Still in a bit of a daze, I shuffled my way into the kitchen. I found my coffee maker sitting at the back of one of my kitchen cupboards, and gently lifted it out, placing it on the counter. I took the coffee out of the refrigerator, opened the canister of Don Francisco's Vanilla Nut, my favorite, and measured out a couple of heaping tablespoons, putting them into a new filter. I filled the trough with water and just as I was about to switch it on, I heard a soft thud. "What the hell was that?" I mumbled, as I turned and looked at the floor.

I stared in disbelief and horror. "How the hell did a frog, the size of my hand, get into my kitchen?" I thought. "Who cared....what the hell was I going to do with him!" I certainly had a variety of choices.

The first of which, was to pick up the little guy, give him a great big kiss and see if he turned into the Prince of Sarasota. With my luck, I felt, he would turn into the typical, Floridian, playboy. Only a Shar Pei puppy, I discovered, has more wrinkles than the average, Sarasota, single male.

My second choice was a better one. I would get him out. I threw a basket over him and on my ceramic tile floor, inched the basket, with my potential Prince Charming under it, to the door. I opened the door, lifted the front of the basket and gave the back a little shove. I watched as Mr. Leap

Frog jumped sideways into the main part of my hallway. He panicked. I panicked. He jumped into my bookcase and I trapped him there with the help of an extra ceramic tile. "Now what?" I thought.

It was still early in the morning, so I went for a walk, through the streets of my condominium area, in the hopes of seeing a real live male, single or otherwise, who would remove my unwanted house guest. "Let him get the warts," I thought.

No luck. I still had the problem. There were few male neighbors around and certainly no one I cared to tell, that I was currently sharing my condominium with another and that "other" was not paying his fair share of the rent.

I went home and checked the bookcase. Poor little guy sat quivering in the corner. I replaced the ceramic tile and went to the community pool for a swim. I hoped I would find someone who found my problem amusing, and would offer to help.

The longer I waited, the more embarrassed I became about asking anyone. He was such a tiny creature. He was not poisonous, nor aggressive, and with pale green skin and a slender body, he was not really offensive in appearance or habits. He definitely had more to fear from me, than I did from him. My decision was made. I walked home purposefully, prepared to resolve the situation, by myself.

I donned rubber gloves, covered the rubber gloves with a plastic bag, opened the front door wide, removed the ceramic tile and peered in. He was either sound asleep, or possibly, in a coma, wedged into the corner of my pale blue bookcase. I surrounded him with the plastic bag, scooped him up into my soft fist, where he immediately came to life. With hearts, his and mine, pounding, I raced out the door, slamming it behind me, opened my hand and watched as he took one small step for man and a giant leap for froggiekind.

I hope I didn't miss my last chance of winning and wooing my Prince Charming?

This book is dedicated to the people in my life who love me unconditionally. They include my brother Nathan, my brother Harry and my sister Mona, who always seems to know when I need that extra bit of encouragement. Dedication includes Joan Aronoff Dressler and Arlene Cohen Kravitz, who have been part of my life since the early years.

This book is also dedicated to the most wonderful person I have ever known:

Paul Gordon Hossack
Always in my heart
February 27, 1940 - June 26, 1992